G000241942

THE FINAL CROSSING

The Final Crossing

Published by The Conrad Press in the United Kingdom 2021

Tel: +44(0)1227 472 874
www.theconradpress.com
info@theconradpress.com

ISBN 978-1-913567-88-0

Copyright © Mike Masson, 2021

The moral right of Mike Masson to be identified as author of this work has been asserted in accordance with the Copyright, Designs and Patents Act 1988.

All rights reserved.

Typesetting and Cover Design by: Charlotte Mouncey, www.bookstyle.co.uk
Cover designed with photos by Ray Harrington, Touann Gatouillat Vergos, Peter F. and Dimitry Anikin all on Unsplash.com
The Conrad Press logo was designed by Maria Priestley.

Printed and bound in Great Britain by Clays Ltd, Elcograf S.p.A.

THE FINAL CROSSING

MIKE MASSON

1

The staccato beep of the pager was loud and insistent.

It jolted him awake and, in his half-conscious state, he somehow knew it must be urgent.

Propping himself up on one elbow, he pressed the light switch on top of his bedside alarm – six thirty. This would not normally be a particularly early start to his day but he hadn't gone to bed until the early hours and had been looking forward to a lie-in until at least half past seven. He stretched his arms as far as he could in the narrow confines of his cabin and switched on the wall light above his pillow.

His clothes lay in a crumpled heap on the floor at the end of his bed, reminding him of how little sleep he had just had. He reached for the phone on the small bedside table and pressed the button marked *Security Control*. The phone was answered immediately by someone he recognised as the duty controller.

'Boss, the captain wants to see you in Conference Room 2 urgently,' he didn't waste time asking why, he would find out soon enough.

'OK, let him know I'll be there in the next ten minutes.'

He replaced the receiver and made his way to the cramped en-suite bathroom. Given the apparent urgency, he didn't feel that he could afford himself the luxury of a shower. Instead, he rinsed his face and upper body in the small sink, ran his electric razor quickly over his stubbly chin and gargled with some mouthwash, hoping to mask the lingering smell of stale alcohol from the previous night's visit to the crew bar.

Calum McIntyre was chief security officer on board the cruise liner Enterprise Endeavour. As such he was classed as a first officer. This afforded him certain privileges not enjoyed by other crew members, one of which was having his own cabin.

He reached into the narrow open fronted wardrobe bolted to the wall at the end of his bed and brought out a freshly laundered uniform of white short sleeved shirt and black trousers. His epaulettes, with their three gold bars and anchor with rope entwined, to signify being a member of the deck department, were already attached to his shirt in readiness for a quick start, which was always a possibility and more often a probability in his job.

Satisfied that he looked at least half presentable, McIntyre left his room, situated midships on Deck 4 just above the waterline and made his way towards the service lift. Entering the lift, he pressed the button for Deck 14. On arrival, he quickly made his way towards Conference Room 2 which was situated at the very front of the ship, three decks above the navigational bridge.

From the moment he had contacted the security control room, McIntyre knew that something potentially serious must have happened.

Each morning at nine o'clock he, along with various other heads of department was required to assemble in the captain's stateroom, situated immediately behind the bridge, for a meeting, commonly referred to as morning prayers. This was usually a very brief meeting to review the events of the past twenty-four hours. Although unspoken, it also gave the captain an opportunity to observe his senior officers together and to reinforce his authority whenever necessary.

The fact that this meeting had been called at such short notice, earlier than normal and in the much larger conference room, meant whatever the problem was, it couldn't wait.

McIntyre reached the conference room, gave a peremptory knock, then entered purposefully. He had a thing about body language and felt the way a person entered a room, especially when others were present, said a lot about them. He quickly noted about a dozen people were already seated around the long oval conference table. The captain was seated at the far end and he motioned towards an empty seat to his right. McIntyre sat down and glanced expectantly at the captain.

Alexander Alexandropoulos, or Captain Alex as he preferred to be known, was Greek. It was a feature of the Enterprise cruise line that virtually all of the senior officers were Greek nationals.

He was a tall, commanding figure, evident even whilst seated and had the swarthy, dark good looks that made the Captain's cocktail parties a delight for many of the female passengers. He was in his mid-forties and obviously kept himself in good shape.

His easy-going manner and laid-back style made him one of the better captains McIntyre had worked under, but today he seemed much more pre-occupied than usual. Captain Alex glanced around the table as if to check that everyone was present. McIntyre did likewise and noted that there were various representatives from the four main departments which comprised the ship's crew.

These were the deck department headed by the captain himself, which included the navigation and security operations. Also present was a representative from the engine department headed by the chief engineer. The environmental department was represented by the environmental officer and the majority of places were occupied by representatives of the hotel department, by far the largest department on the ship, headed by the hotel director. The cruise director, who came within the remit of the hotel department was also present.

Having apparently satisfied himself that everyone was there, Captain Alex took a sip of water and cleared his throat. In his heavily accented English, he began.

'First of all, ladies and gentlemen, thank you all for getting here at such short notice. I'll come straight to the point. At approximately six o'clock this morning we received a report that one of our passengers has gone missing. The person in question is a female aged forty-six, a UK national, by the name of Anne Ebsworth. She is travelling with her husband who is disabled and wheelchair bound.

According to the husband, they had dressed for dinner last night and were intending to go down to the dining room at around half past seven. The husband however said he wasn't feeling very well and preferred to remain in their stateroom, which is 1249, Deck 10 starboard and intended to order room service later on if he felt better.

As he was very tired from his medication, he said he told his wife she should dine alone and to the best of his recollection he thinks she left the stateroom around seven forty-five. She hasn't been seen since.

As you all know, last night was the first formal night on this cruise and the husband said his wife was wearing a royal blue, floor- length dress with a strap over the left shoulder and a silver-sequinned bolero style jacket over the top. She was also carrying a small clutch bag which closely resembled the jacket in colour. Hopefully before you leave the room, or at least as soon as they are available, I will issue each of you with an enlargement of the latest photo of the missing person, taken at security check- in prior to her boarding the ship.

It is also possible she may have been photographed by the ship's photographers immediately prior to embarkation. If so, we may be able to get a more natural image of her.

With the husband's permission, we have already conducted a search of their stateroom and the immediate vicinity, but the missing passenger definitely wasn't there. Nobody has spoken to the husband at any length, other than to establish that his wife definitely does not seem to have returned to her stateroom between the time she was last seen to have left and the time he reported her missing this morning.' Captain Alex paused, before continuing.

'You will all be familiar with the search protocol to be followed in cases like this and I want each head of department to take personal responsibility for ensuring that the full and proper procedures are carried out. It goes without saying that the search should be as discreet as possible as the last thing we want to do is spread alarm amongst the passengers.'

At this point, a member of the purser's staff knocked and entered the room carrying a pile of buff folders which were quickly deposited with the captain. He glanced quickly through the top folder and continued.

'Fortunately, we have a couple of very good images of the missing passenger here, together with an up-to-date copy of the search protocol. Please take one each and let's get started.

We will set up an incident room here in the meantime. Mr Konstantinos our Staff Captain will assume overall responsibility as Gold Control, Mr McIntyre our CSO will be Silver and Bronze Control will be our Safety Officer Mr Samaras. We will establish a dedicated telephone line within this room, through which all communications must be passed.

Do not, I repeat do *not*, convey any messages regarding this incident over the shipboard radios. With a little luck we will find the missing lady alive and well, but we have to be prepared for an alternative outcome. Are there any questions?'

Practically everyone round the table was probably thinking along similar lines, but McIntyre jumped in first.

'Presumably we don't have any evidence to suggest it yet, but there must be at least a possibility that she may have fallen overboard. Have you considered turning back and initiating a search along the route we have travelled between the time she was last seen and the time that she was reported missing?'

All eyes were on the captain, anticipating his reply. Captain Alex took his time before speaking again.

'This is a very difficult decision for me to have to make. Given our position from the nearest landfall between approximately seven forty-five last night and now and the current sea conditions, even if we had proof that she had fallen overboard, her chances of survival would be extremely minimal.

I have discussed it with my bridge team and on balance we

can see no merit in retracing our route. The details have been passed to all possible resources via a PAN-PAN alert and if we can confirm quickly that she has fallen overboard, I'm sure a search will be conducted along our route by the relevant authorities, but in the meantime, we will concentrate the search onboard.'

McIntyre knew that despite this brief and concise response, the captain would have done much soul searching before reaching his decision. Only time would tell if he had called it right.

Captain Alex rose to his feet to signify that the meeting was closed and finished by saying,

'Let's get to work everyone and keep the Control Room informed of the progress of the search in each of your departments. Good luck.'

He motioned to McIntyre, the staff captain and the safety officer to remain behind as everyone else left the room. The Gold, Silver and Bronze command system was one which was used extensively by many police forces and in the military, to assist in the running of major incidents and had been adopted by the cruise line.

Although captain of the ship and therefore the most senior officer on board, Captain Alex preferred to keep an overview of proceedings from a distance and obviously felt that overall command for this incident should rest with his deputy, the staff captain, who was the second most senior officer on the ship. The selection of McIntyre and the safety officer as Silver and Bronze respectively was a natural choice, as this type of incident fell within their remit.

Having satisfied himself that the incident control team were fully briefed and resourced, Captain Alex left the room to return to the navigational bridge. At exactly ten o'clock, as was the case every morning, seven days a week, he would conduct a short address to all passengers and crew over the ship's broadcasting system, giving details such as the ship's position, speed, distance from land, ocean depth and weather conditions and any other information which he considered relevant.

Today this may have to include an appeal for assistance in case anyone, passengers or crew alike, had seen anything of the missing passenger. In the meantime, he hoped that this would not be necessary.

The search had begun.

2

It had just gone four o'clock on Friday afternoon when Anne Ebsworth left her office, located in a nondescript industrial estate in a small town in Kent, around thirty-five miles from central London.

It was early October and it was raining lightly, making it seem dark earlier than usual. She hurried towards the car park which was by now almost empty. She hunched her shoulders against the rain being driven on a stiff breeze and silently wished she had parked closer to the entrance to her office when she had turned up for work earlier that morning. After all, there had been plenty of spaces, as she had been the first to arrive as usual.

She pressed the button on her remote-control key and sighed with relief as her vehicle's sidelights pierced the gathering gloom. As she settled into the driver's seat, she glanced back at her office which was now in darkness. Even the boss had left early, apparently happy in the knowledge that the ever-dependable Anne would take care of locking up. She didn't immediately start the engine and drive off however.

There was much on her mind and she knew that before too much longer, the juggling act her life had become, would come crashing down around her.

She sat for a few minutes, trying to clear her head for the

short journey home through the rush hour traffic. She stared silently ahead, as the eerie glow of the car park lights cast an orange sheen into the half-light of dusk.

Anne had worked at Ace Valves, a small light engineering company, for almost twenty-five years. She had started as an accounts clerk when the company was in its infancy and had only a handful of employees, herself included.

By virtue of sheer hard work and a little luck in securing valuable contracts however, the owners had built the business into a very successful enterprise, with an annual turnover in excess of seven figures and now employing around forty staff.

Along the way, Anne had elected to grow with the business and over the years had gained her accountancy qualifications, enabling her to become the company's financial controller. Part of the company's success lay in her extremely astute handling of contract negotiations relating to new business.

In view of her undoubted ability and total dedication, the owners were more than happy to leave the financial aspect of running the company in Anne's seemingly capable hands, whilst they concentrated on the core business of engineering.

She was an unremarkable woman in many ways.

Married to Dean for almost twenty years, she had always seemed to be cast in his shadow, the subordinate partner in the union- at least that was how it seemed to the outside world.

Unbeknown to most however, the dynamic of their relationship had changed greatly since Dean's accident five years previously. Physically, she was attractive, but in an understated sort of way. Around five feet six inches tall and slightly built, she certainly didn't stand out in a crowd. Neither did the way she dressed draw any undue attention.

At work she normally wore a conservative combination of blouse and skirt, rarely in any colour which could be termed vibrant and occasionally a simple dress. Her hair was naturally an unusual russet colour, which she disliked intensely. As a result, it was permanently dyed blonde.

Her hair was one of her most striking features. It was fashionably cut in a short bob, expertly layered at the back and with a longer sweep at the front, reaching almost down to her chin. Even to an outsider it was obvious that her hair was professionally styled.

At work, she wore a minimal amount of jewellery, mostly gold. She had a liking for expensive handbags, Michael Kors being a particular favourite. This however, was one of her few ostentations.

Anne had an extremely pale complexion, which she did little to hide with make-up and just a hint of freckles on her face. Despite her forty-six years, her face was relatively smooth and unlined, no doubt as a result of her skin texture precluding over exposure to strong sunlight over the years. Her green eyes occasionally sparkled when she smiled, which wasn't often. There was a certain aura that radiated from those eyes; regret, guilt, sadness, it was difficult to fathom.

After a short period of silent contemplation, Anne started up her car and headed towards the mini roundabout that connected the industrial estate to the town's arterial network.

She knew that all her concentration should now be directed to navigating the heavy rush-hour traffic, but still, she couldn't stop her mind from wandering. She should be happy- after all she was just about to start her two-week holiday, a re-positioning cruise to the Caribbean, but inside she felt a sense of dread which could easily rise to panic if she didn't control her rapid breathing.

After the third or fourth oncoming vehicle had flashed its headlights in her direction, Anne suddenly realised that she hadn't switched on her own headlights and, as it was now raining heavily, visibility was poor.

With great difficulty, she tried to clear her mind of the jumble of confused thoughts and concentrate on the job in hand- getting home safely.

Since their marriage, Anne and Dean had moved several times within the town where they were both born and brought up, each move being to a more upmarket location.

There seemed to be nothing remarkable about this as Anne's position at Ace Valves allowed for advancement, although Dean was now registered disabled and unable to undertake any form of work.

Home was a half hour drive away but tonight, because of the traffic conditions and her confused state, it took nearer to forty-five minutes.

Eventually and with a sense of relief, Anne pulled off the main carriageway into her street, a neat tree-lined avenue of detached, period houses.

From the street, most of the houses, but theirs in particular, had what estate agents would describe as kerb appeal. The front garden of the four-bedroom house was a generous ten metres deep and laid mainly to lawn, with triple Old Yorkshire stone circles as the centrepiece.

In the middle of the stone circles stood a metre-high granite effect statuette of Eros, complete with iconic wings and bow. The lawn was surrounded by a narrow shrub border. A paved driveway ran along one side of the house leading to a double garage at the rear of the property.

Because of the length of the drive, it was possible to comfortably accommodate at least three or four vehicles. Already parked outside one of the garage entrances was an electric-blue, three litre Range Rover Vogue. Anne parked her VW Golf alongside it and switched off the ignition.

She felt a wave of exhaustion wash over her as she gathered up her belongings. She had certainly had a challenging week at work, particularly in the lead up to her holiday, but this wasn't the only reason for the feeling of utter desolation she felt at that moment.

There were three entrances to the house; one via an enclosed front porch, a side door leading directly from the drive and a rear patio door facing the back garden, which extended almost forty metres out from the back wall of the house.

Anne headed towards the side door which was the only one of the three without a disabled access ramp leading to it. As she fumbled in her handbag for her housekeys, a security light positioned above the door suddenly illuminated the gathering gloom.

After a juggling act with her handbag, some files from work and a couple of bags of shopping from a lunchtime trip to the supermarket, Anne finally opened the door and stepped inside.

As she closed and double locked the door behind her, she noticed that the house appeared to be in almost complete darkness. This was not particularly concerning to her, but as was her habit, she called out, 'Dean, I'm home,' but got no response.

A short corridor from the side entrance led into the main entrance hallway which was wide and spacious. Several doors led off the hallway leading to a cloakroom, downstairs toilet, kitchen, dining room/conservatory, main lounge and a master bedroom with en-suite facilities and walk in wardrobe. A modern staircase with open-tread wooden steps and steel and glass sides led up to a galleried landing on the first floor.

Switching on the floor lamp in the hall-way, Anne headed towards the main lounge. As she had expected, Dean lay sprawled across one of two couches, snoring gently. On a low coffee table beside the couch, she noted the pill container with multiple sections to accommodate his different types of medication.

Also on the table was a glass tumbler with about an inch of clear liquid at the bottom. Approaching quietly, she took a small sip from it. The taste was unmistakeable as it appeared to be almost neat spirit – vodka.

The opposite wall was dominated by a seventy-seven-inch plasma TV screen which flickered silently in the semi-darkness.

A wheelchair was positioned at the head of the couch. Anne pushed Dean's legs further on to the couch and perched at his feet. As she sat looking at him, she felt a mixture of emotions; pity, anger, revulsion.

To the outside world she appeared to have everything, despite Dean's disability, but no one could have guessed the depths of her loneliness and inner turmoil at that precise moment. In the gathering darkness, silent tears coursed down her face.

After a few minutes, Anne got up and switched on some soft lighting around the lounge. It was time to waken Dean, but this would be no easy task as she knew from past experience.

After much coaxing, Dean sparked slowly into life, his bloodshot eyes squinting in the dim lighting as he attempted to push himself upright. Anne bent to help him, but he angrily pushed her away, cursing beneath his breath.

His upper body seemed to respond to his attempts to raise himself to a sitting position, but his legs hung limply and did not respond. After several minutes, involving much effort and an equal amount of profanity, Dean was finally sitting upright.

'What sort of day have you had, darling?' Anne asked.

Dean's response was to grab the TV remote control, turn up the volume and appear to concentrate his attention on the programme that had been silently running in the background. Anne knew how the remainder of the day would play out.

Anne changed out of her work clothing and packed a small sports holdall with her training kit. She knew from long experience what sort of mood Dean was likely to be in for the rest of the evening and any attempt at holding a meaningful conversation would be wasted.

As a form of stress relief initially, Anne had joined a local gym, which she attended regularly two or three times a week. Tonight, she was in need of a visit, not only to maintain her already trim physique, but also to attend to more pressing matters.

3

Dean Ebsworth was a couple of years younger than his wife. They had both attended the same high school, but had not been romantically involved in any way during that period.

Growing up in a small provincial town however, it was inevitable that they would bump into each other from time to time after leaving school.

Nevertheless, when they started seeing each other in their early twenties, it came as something of a surprise to most of their family and friends. In many ways they were polar opposites.

Dean grew up on a council estate in one of the rougher parts of town. One of six siblings, he had left school with few qualifications. He was the product of a broken home, as his father - a man with an eye for the ladies, particularly barmaids - had left home when Dean was just a toddler.

As a result, he grew up with a lack of male role models to give him stability and direction in life.

He had always managed to find work however, mainly within the construction industry.

Just short of six feet tall, the rigours of his job gave him an imposing physique in his younger years, which also led to trouble. Dean possessed a short fuse and it needed little in the way of provocation for him to resort to violence.

This had led to several brushes with the police and a couple of convictions for disorderly conduct and minor assault.

Despite all this however, his strong work ethic kept him largely on the straight and narrow. Like many young men, Dean began to settle down as he neared his mid-twenties, although he retained an independent streak, which could be easily mistaken for arrogance.

Over time however, he established a reputation for reliability within the construction industry and eventually secured regular employment as a scaffolder.

Starting both metaphorically and figuratively at the bottom, Dean acquired the skills necessary to become good at his trade and eventually went on to manage the small scaffolding company in his own right. As events would prove however, his involvement in this venture was to prove both a blessing and a curse.

Anne's path in life had followed a very different course. As an only child, she was the apple of her parents' eye, particularly her father's. He was an electrical engineer and her mother a midwife, although both were now retired.

Her upbringing was solidly middle class, with home being a three-bedroom semi-detached house a few streets away from where Dean lived.

She had been a girl guide in her teens and her parents indulged her love of horses, taking her to riding lessons every weekend. At least once a year the family would spend a holiday abroad, usually the Greek islands or Florida.

Anne had stayed on at high school, achieving several passes at A-level and had high hopes of becoming a veterinary nurse, probably because of her equine activities. Her academic qualifications did not match her career ambitions however, something which took her some time to come to terms with.

After leaving school, she had a succession of temporary jobs through an employment agency, either as an administrative assistant or accounts clerk.

It was through the latter of these assignments that Anne started working at Ace Valves. She was a reliable and conscientious worker, something which was quickly recognised and appreciated by the management of the fledgling company and within a year she had left the agency and became a full-time employee.

As an only child, Anne tended to be a bit of a loner and had never had a serious boyfriend until she and Dean started seeing each other.

Quite what attracted each to the other was something of a mystery to all who knew them. Anne's parents in particular were less than enthusiastic when they announced their engagement. They could see however, that despite the obvious difference in their personalities and upbringing, the couple appeared happy, and gave their blessing to the marriage.

Married life had its occasional challenges for the couple, mainly caused by Dean's controlling temperament and the fact that he often worked away.

After several years of trying to start a family together, Anne was given the devastating news that she was unable to conceive.

More than ever, after this shock diagnosis, both seemed to concentrate more on work, spending less time in each other's company. Despite this however, they appeared reasonably happy.

Her colleagues at work did notice however, that on several occasions, Anne had taken two or three days off sick and usually on her return they had noticed bruising around her face or arms, which she tried to conceal with make-up or long sleeves. She never commented on this, nor did anyone ask.

4

On Saturday morning, Anne busied herself packing and preparing for the cruise. On her return from the gym the previous evening, she found that Dean had already gone to bed and appeared to be asleep. Today, he was up and about early and was in an extremely cheerful mood.

Anne had become used to these mood swings. After all, his life had changed dramatically in the past five years and she had learned to make allowances for his erratic behaviour. As she sat nursing a cup of coffee in the kitchen, her mind drifted back to that fateful day, when both their lives had changed forever.

It was late one afternoon and she was still at work when she was called out of a meeting.

As she walked into reception, she noticed two uniformed police officers hovering in the background. Their expressions were grim and Anne sensed immediately that they were the bearers of bad news. The younger of the two officers shifted uncomfortably before speaking.

'Are you Mrs Anne Ebsworth?' She nodded in confirmation.

'I think you'd better take a seat,' continued the officer.

Anne's immediate thoughts were that something had happened to one or both of her parents.

'Your husband Dean has had a very serious accident at work

I'm afraid. I don't have too many details at the moment but there's been a scaffolding collapse on the multi-storey building he was working on. He was trapped for a while but he's now been freed and taken to hospital. We don't have an update on his condition but we'll take you up there now if you wish.'

Anne gave an involuntary shudder as she recalled arriving at the hospital. She was ushered into a private room where she waited for what seemed like an eternity, before a doctor in theatre scrubs entered.

Within minutes she was taken through to a small recovery ward where she caught her first sight of her husband since the accident.

He lay on a stretcher-type bed, similar to a body board, with his head held firmly in place in a neck brace. A broad Velcro strap was wrapped across his chest, to inhibit movement. A plethora of tubes and catheters were in-situ in his head and upper limbs, all linked to various machines.

Dean appeared unconscious, but Anne remembered being surprised that he didn't show any obvious signs of injury, apart from a few deep lacerations to his shoulders and upper torso. This briefly gave her hope that his condition was not as serious as she had been led to believe, but her optimism was short lived.

In the days immediately following the accident, Dean drifted in and out of consciousness. He required a ventilator to breathe and remained heavily sedated. He was a big man but it was heart breaking for Anne to see how helpless he looked.

Gradually however he began to come around and become aware of his surroundings. It was then that the full impact of the accident became apparent to both of them.

It was explained by the doctors that the most serious injury sustained by Dean was to his spine. Nerves in his lower spinal cord had been severed, resulting in complete paralysis below the site of the injury.

In Dean's case, this meant he was now classed as paraplegic. He was transferred to a specialist hospital, where he remained for several months and it was during that time that his paraplegia was confirmed.

Dean no longer had any movement from the waist down, an outcome which was almost certainly irreversible.

Anne thought back to her life during this period. It hadn't been much of a life at all, merely an exercise in survival, involving work, hospital visits and making plans for their future together, a future which was to become totally transformed. Dean had not exactly been a model husband before the accident, but he was generally dependable and a provider, attributes which Anne valued in their relationship. They now had to face a future together where Anne had to assume the role as the main carer and provider.

After his eventual release from hospital, Dean returned to the marital home which had been hurriedly adapted in his absence, to make it wheelchair friendly. This was not the house that they currently lived in, but a much more modest two-bedroom semi.

Understandably, Dean found it hard to come to terms with his new found condition. He had gone from being an active and physically robust man, doing a job he enjoyed in an outdoor environment, to an impotent cripple, confined indoors.

Added to this, he was in constant pain and needed to take a cocktail of powerful drugs which resulted in massive mood swings. Initially he sank into a deep depression but eventually, with the help of counselling and much patience from Anne, he seemed to become more accepting of his new status in life.

Despite his lower limb paralysis, he had regained almost normal movement in his upper body. His once powerful physique had been greatly reduced by the trauma he had undergone in the previous months however and to an alpha-male like Dean, this was the hardest aspect of all to come to terms with.

For Dean, life had never been easy and he embarked on a punishing schedule of strengthening exercises in an effort to regain some of the physical attributes that had once defined him.

Within a relatively short time he had rebuilt his upper body to the point where anyone, not being aware of his condition, would look at him, especially in a seated position and think that he was a body builder.

Despite all this however, Dean continued to experience bouts of deep depression which sometimes manifested itself in violence, usually directed towards Anne. In addition to his prescription drug intake, Anne gradually began to notice that he was getting access to alcohol, brought to him she suspected, by one of his brothers.

Dean's good humour continued, as Anne carried on with the preparations for their cruise. Of course, she had expected this - who could blame him? It would be a welcome break from the monotony of his everyday life.

Prior to his accident, they had never cruised before, but this was now to be their third in the space of five years.

Both had doubts about cruising at first. Dean, because he had feared that his disability would limit his ability to enjoy himself and people would probably feel sorry for him. This was something which he always hated, but despite these reservations he had thoroughly embraced the experience and had become a cruise convert.

Anne had similar misgivings, particularly regarding Dean, but for her the whole cruise scenario induced an altogether different range of feelings. It was an escape for them both and she enjoyed the break from normality, but there was something that was troubling her, particularly in the lead up to this cruise.

Despite her conflicting feelings however, Anne always felt a strange surge of exhilaration prior to leaving on these trips. She couldn't define it, but she knew for that short period in her life, she could be someone other than her normal self; she could enjoy and express herself.

Physically, she underwent something of a metamorphosis. There were hair, nail and spa treatments to look forward to whilst on board and the range of outfits she brought along she could never wear at home.

Although not normally one to express his feelings towards her, apart from with sporadic violence, Anne felt Dean secretly liked the change that occurred in her during these times.

She could tell he was excited and looking forward to the break and this gave her a warm glow, because in her heart all she wanted was to regain some of the old spark that they had enjoyed at the outset of their marriage.

The rest of that day was spent by both in eager anticipation of the trip to come, with Anne busily selecting a range of glamorous outfits for the evenings which lay ahead, particularly the formal nights.

Packing complete, the couple retired early, although both were too full of anticipation to sleep very well.

5

It was still dark when Anne placed the last suitcase in the rear of the Range Rover and checked that the house was locked and secure.

It had just gone seven-thirty when she turned out of their driveway and began the short journey along the south coast to Southampton.

She turned the radio on to one of the easy listening channels. Before long, both she and Dean were singing along to one of their favourite songs from the early days of their marriage.

Moments like these brought feelings of nostalgia, as they didn't happen very often and reminded her of the way their relationship used to be.

After a pleasant but uneventful journey, they finally arrived in Southampton.

Anne was surprised to find that even mid-morning on a Sunday, the traffic was nose to tail as they approached the City Cruise Terminal, but their ship wasn't due to sail until four o'clock that afternoon, so they were in no rush.

As they passed through the dock gates, the gleaming white hull of the Enterprise Endeavour, which they had seen in the distance, now loomed before them.

They moved forward slowly until they were alongside the

massive vessel herself, so tall you had to crane your neck to see the top deck.

Anne cast her mind back to her maiden trip, when she had seen a cruise liner at close quarters for the first time, but even now her heart began to race at the latest sighting.

The quay alongside the ship was a hive of activity, with fork-lift trucks swarming like ants around numerous supply vehicles and the open cargo doors of the ship.

On some of the upper decks, seamen in white boiler suits hung precariously from cradles attached to gantries on the ship's side.

Some were applying paint to the hull whilst others were using powerful jet washes on the numerous windows and paint-work. Even in port, it seemed, the crew were working flat out.

As they neared the entrance to the modern terminal build-ing, a yellow-jacketed traffic marshal glanced at the sticker prominently displayed on their windscreen, before directing them into a bay marked *wheelchair assistance*.

From this point onwards, the process of boarding commenced with practiced efficiency. Porters quickly unloaded their luggage, which already bore pre-printed labels with their stateroom number and a uniformed driver removed the vehicle to a secure parking area on the dockside.

With Dean settled comfortably into his customised wheel-chair, they were quickly ushered through the check in and security clearance procedures, before being issued with their sea passes, which would be used as identification on entering and leaving the ship, as keys to their stateroom and to pay for any goods or services on board.

The final stage of boarding saw them reach the bottom of

the gangway where the ship's photographers were waiting to take pictures of each guest as they boarded.

Despite this being the first of many opportunities for the cruise line to earn revenue, the photographers weren't pushy, which resulted in the couple agreeing to have their pictures taken.

Wheelchair users received priority boarding, which meant the couple were at the top of the ship's gangway barely less than fifteen minutes after entering the terminal.

As they reached the entrance to the ship, their sea passes were scanned by a member of security staff, before they were ushered inside. A short line-up of beaming staff welcomed them on board, before they were each offered a glass of complementary champagne.

For purely commercial reasons, cruise lines generally board their passengers on one of the decks bearing the retail and entertainment outlets and this was no exception.

Having been on a cruise ship before, the couple had passed the stage of being dazzled by the opulence that lay before them, but they still took time to gaze around at the glitz and glamour of their new surroundings.

Anne's eyes were drawn upwards to the huge chandeliers that hung above the central atrium and to the glass sided lifts that soared up and down between decks.

Since they had boarded early, their stateroom wasn't ready for immediate occupation and having been advised on embarkation that there was a greater than usual number of wheelchair users on this cruise, Anne knew that they may have a considerable time to wait.

Dean took himself off in his wheelchair to play the slot

machines in the casino area, whilst Anne headed for one of the speciality coffee bars. She was keen to encourage time apart from the outset, particularly on this cruise.

As had often been the case during previous cruises, Dean enjoyed some success in the casino and joined Anne in the coffee bar after an hour or so.

Both were eager to explore the ship but experienced enough to know that on embarkation day this was inadvisable, particularly for someone with mobility problems, as all the public areas were mobbed with passengers.

At Dean's suggestion, they moved from the coffee bar to the Schooner Inn, an English themed pub on Deck 5, to await the announcement that the staterooms were ready for occupation. Whilst sitting there, Dean noticed that Anne looked unusually nervous and uneasy.

'What's up with you?' he finally asked.

'It's nothing... I think I'm just a bit stressed out from the early start and the drive and everything.'

Eventually they made their way to their stateroom where their luggage was already waiting outside the door. Almost immediately a small, uniformed Filipino male appeared beside them.

'Good afternoon sir, madam,' he said before giving a small bow of greeting.

'Welcome aboard. My name is Angelo and I'm your room steward. Let me help you with your luggage and if there's anything at all you need whilst you're on board please don't hesitate to ask.'

Anne made a mental note to tip him early in the cruise, as this usually seemed to guarantee first class service.

She was not disappointed on entering the stateroom.

Being wheelchair compliant, it was spacious and well appointed, with twin beds, a two-seater settee and coffee table, a large built-in wardrobe and a side unit affixed to one wall, containing a safe and fully stocked mini-bar. An en-suite shower room and toilet completed the accommodation.

Floor-to-ceiling glass sliding doors led out onto a large balcony. A bottle of champagne sat chilling in an ice bucket on the coffee table.

Anne could tell Dean was eager to open the bottle, despite the fact they'd already had a couple of drinks in the Schooner Inn, but she knew they had to attend the mandatory lifeboat drill before the ship set sail.

Besides, they had two weeks ahead of them and had paid for a premium drinks package, so the champagne could wait a little longer.

After familiarising themselves with their stateroom, the couple made their way to their designated lifeboat station for the pre-sailing drill.

Nearly every passenger hated having to take part in this, but non-attendance could mean passage being denied.

The muster station was always crowded and uncomfortable and both passengers and crew alike simply wanted the process to be completed as quickly as possible.

At the conclusion of the drill, Anne asked Dean if he wanted to go to one of the upper decks to watch as the ship sailed away from Southampton.

She had sailed from Southampton before and, weather permitting, enjoyed being on the upper deck as they started the two-hour journey down the Solent, before reaching the open waters of the English Channel.

Dean however preferred to return to the Schooner Inn. Anne wasn't disappointed at being left alone, as apart from the view, she had other issues to deal with now that they were underway.

6

By mid-afternoon on Wednesday, it had become obvious to Calum McIntyre the search for the missing person wasn't going to produce a positive outcome any time soon.

The department heads had all reported back to the incident room they had drawn a blank in their respective searches.

Examination of CCTV footage throughout the ship, in particular the upper and outside decks, was continuing, but so far nothing unusual had been observed.

McIntyre was as certain as he could be at this stage that the missing passenger had not fallen overboard and the answer to her disappearance somehow lay within the ship itself.

A meeting had been arranged between Captain Alex and the Incident Control Team for four o'clock to discuss progress.

In the meantime, McIntyre returned briefly to his cabin to freshen up, as it promised to be a long day. He had a feeling, a sixth-sense almost, that this wasn't going to be a straightforward investigation.

As he prepared for the meeting with the captain, McIntyre's mind drifted back to the start of his career as a ship security officer.

He was born in a small town on the Isle of Harris, off the North West coast of Scotland.

He came from a family of seafarers. Both his grandfathers had been fishermen and his father had served for many years in the Merchant Navy.

As a young man growing up, McIntyre had spent as much time messing about on boats as he had on dry land and listened with fascination to the tales of his elders.

Until his early teens, his first language was Gaelic and even now, he spoke with the soft highland lilt peculiar to Gaelic speakers.

Because of his upbringing, it was assumed he would also pursue a career at sea, but an altogether different career path unexpectedly beckoned.

During his last year at high school, he attended a careers information event where one of the presentations was by a small recruitment team from the London Metropolitan Police.

McIntyre was fascinated by the presentation and the endless opportunities it seemed to offer.

His mind was made up and shortly after leaving school, he joined the Metropolitan Police Cadet Corps, which was a stepping stone to joining as a fully-fledged police officer.

Arriving in London was a complete culture shock to the young McIntyre. It was as different to island life as it was possible to imagine.

For the first few weeks, he experienced intense bouts of homesickness, but these soon abated as he threw himself into the challenges of life as a police cadet.

For the first time in his life, he met fellow cadets from all parts of the country, which was a refreshing change to the insularity he had experienced at home.

Despite being so far from home and out of his comfort zone,

McIntyre excelled as a cadet and before he left to enrol as a trainee police constable, he had won the Baton of Honour, as top cadet in his intake.

After passing out of Hendon Police Training College, McIntyre was posted to a central London police station as a probationary constable. His beat included Soho and it was here he very quickly realised he had made the right career choice.

Within a relatively short time he went from being a naïve islander to a streetwise cop. He worked and played hard and very early in his service, he knew his career ambitions lay in the Criminal Investigation Department as a detective.

Having eventually been accepted into the CID, McIntyre's career saw a steady progression through the ranks, until he eventually retired as a Detective Chief Inspector after thirty years' service.

For McIntyre, the job always came first and this was largely instrumental in the breakdown of both of his marriages.

He hadn't yet turned fifty on retirement from the police and his divorces had hit him hard financially. He knew he would have to find other employment, but after the variety and excitement of his police career, he knew it would take something special to hold his interest.

A chance encounter with a former colleague, who was already working within the cruise industry, alerted him to the possibilities of a new career which suited his circumstances.

It had taken a long time, but it somehow seemed destined that a man who had grown up in a seafaring community had finally set sail.

McIntyre made his way to the Incident Room on Deck 14 for

the meeting with the captain and was first to arrive. He was joined promptly on the stroke of four o'clock by Captain Alex, Staff Captain Andreas Konstantinos and Georgios Samaras, the Safety Officer. Captain Alex opened the conversation without any preamble.

'I take it, gentlemen, we haven't made any progress in locating the missing passenger?' The others nodded in agreement.

'I understand from the updates you've already given me the ship has been thoroughly searched throughout the course of the day and nothing has been found to explain her disappearance.

Your examination of the CCTV footage would also suggest she doesn't appear to have gone overboard.

We will now have to conduct a full investigation into the circumstances of her disappearance. I will leave it in your hands to do whatever it takes to bring this to a satisfactory conclusion. If there are any additional resources you need, let me know immediately.'

Prior to embarkation at Southampton, McIntyre had made an interesting and welcome discovery.

One of the guest speakers on the cruise was none other than a former colleague with whom he had worked on numerous murder investigations, when both were based in an Area Major Investigation Team in the Met.

Mike Lewis had been a detective superintendent, which meant he was McIntyre's boss. Both men had worked well together and a strong professional relationship had carried over into an enduring friendship.

They had met briefly a couple of times since leaving Southampton and a longer, more convivial meeting was planned when both could fit it into their busy schedules.

McIntyre considered there was nothing to lose by asking.

'Captain, you are probably aware that one of the guest speakers on the cruise, Mike Lewis, is a retired police officer. He and I are former colleagues and I hold him in extremely high regard as an investigator.

I know it's probably an unusual request, but as these are unusual circumstances, is there any possibility that we can call upon his assistance to get to the bottom of this? I'm fairly certain that he will agree to help out if asked.'

Captain Alex appeared to ponder for a moment or two - at least he wasn't dismissing the request out of hand.

'I'll have to run this past our head office before I can give you the go ahead but personally it seems like a good idea to me. I'll let you know as soon possible. Good luck gentlemen, I'll leave you to it.'

As soon as the captain had left the room, McIntyre could sense his two colleagues were keen for him to assume the lead role in the investigation.

They were seamen first and foremost not investigators and knew all about his police background. Just to make sure however, he checked with both that they were happy for him to formulate a plan of action.

Both men readily agreed. McIntyre began considering his options. The first issue that would arise would be one of jurisdiction, in the event of foul play being detected.

They were embarked on a sixteen-day cruise to reposition the ship from the European to the Caribbean circuit.

Around the time the passenger went missing, they were on day two of seven consecutive sea days, before reaching the first landfall in the United States.

This would have placed them slightly north west of the Azores and well into international waters.

The Enterprise Endeavour was an American-owned ship and its final destination was Fort Lauderdale in Florida.

There was no question at that point, that jurisdiction for any investigation lay with the captain of the ship and now by delegation, with McIntyre himself.

Far from feeling the weight of responsibility, he relished the challenge, even more so when he learned within the hour that agreement had been reached for Mike Lewis to join his team.

Every cruise, particularly ones with multiple sea days, has at least two cruise lecturers on board, catering for two main types of lecture; *destination lectures* and *specialist subjects*.

Essentially, each lecturer would be expected to deliver one fifty-minute lecture each sea day, covering both criteria.

Lewis had been hired primarily as a specialist subject lecturer, particularly as one of his major investigations as a Senior Investigating Officer had involved the murder of a well-known female TV personality in London.

This particular case had received wide media coverage throughout the UK and beyond and hearing details of the investigation first hand would have been of particular interest to the mainly British passengers on board.

Mike Lewis was a confident public speaker and knew he had to be on these cruises.

In his experience, the audiences could be very unforgiving. Any mistakes made by the lecturer could expect to be punished severely, by embarrassing and none too subtle declamations by some passengers who frequented cruises, possibly just for that pleasure it seemed.

He was also extremely reliable, which made him very popular with the entertainment's officers, who lived in fear and dread of a performer or lecturer not turning up at the right port on the right day.

Personality wise, Lewis was a totally different character to McIntyre.

Born and brought up in Devon, the son of a vicar father and school teacher mother, he had joined the Metropolitan Police in his mid-twenties, but his formidable intellect and leadership qualities saw him rise quickly through the ranks.

Unlike McIntyre, he had been married only once, a union which had endured for over thirty years. In his retirement, he knew that he had many stories to tell and this, combined with the love of travel that he and his wife enjoyed, made cruise ship lecturing an obvious choice.

Although unassuming and slightly refined by nature, Lewis quickly realised the need to adopt a lecturer's persona.

He learnt how to be idiosyncratic without being 'camp'. He took to wearing a bow tie, white jacket, a flower in his lapel and an immaculate haircut and set out to be more British than the British - the Americans in particular loved it.

He made many friends and acquaintances, some becoming alcoholics, as the life of a lecturer became intensely monotonous for certain individuals, surrounded by a sea of alcohol and ample free time. As a student of human nature however, he found it to be an unparalleled experience.

Fortunately, on this cruise Lewis was travelling alone. Therefore, he was surprised and delighted to receive the call from McIntyre to join him in the incident room.

After hearing a brief outline of the facts, Lewis accepted the invitation to join the team with alacrity, particularly since he would still be able to honour his commitments as a lecturer.

'Just like old times, guv,' said McIntyre as they got the investigation underway.

'Yes, except this time, you're the one in charge,' replied Lewis with a grin.

7

The team got to work straight away. It had been almost twenty-four hours since the last sighting of Anne Ebsworth and there were now serious concerns about her possible fate.

Both Lewis and McIntyre knew the early stages of an investigation such as this were crucial.

Every hour that passed might lead to the loss of vital evidence and compromise the missing person's safety, in the increasingly unlikely event that she was still alive.

'I think the first thing we need to do is speak to the husband at some length to try to find out what may have happened,' Lewis suggested.

Even though they were both now retired, the dynamic of their previous police relationship persisted and McIntyre was happy for his former boss to take the lead, despite his earlier assertion to the contrary.

'Before we do that, is it possible to have him moved to a different stateroom, so we can examine the one they're in at the moment without interference?'

Both McIntyre and Lewis knew the stateroom was a potential crime scene.

The move was easily arranged and within a short time, Dean Ebsworth found himself in an upgraded stateroom, a couple of decks higher up the ship. After being given a short time to settle in, he was joined by Lewis and McIntyre.

Both men immediately formed the impression that Dean was genuinely upset by his wife's unexplained disappearance.

Being seasoned investigators, they had learned over the years to interpret an interviewee's demeanour, within a very short time of meeting.

Whilst Lewis gently probed, McIntyre made notes of the conversation in his incident report book. As a backup, he had covertly switched on the record facility on his mobile phone.

'I appreciate this is a very difficult time for you,' said Lewis by way of opening, 'but our one and only concern is for the welfare of your wife and finding her as quickly as we possibly can.

I apologise if some of the questions I'm going to ask you may seem personal, but it's important we get the full picture and we'd very much appreciate your full co-operation in trying to find out as much as possible about the circumstances of her disappearance.'

Whilst speaking to him, both men closely examined Dean's physical appearance, without making it appear particularly obvious.

They noted that although he was wheelchair bound and obviously of limited mobility, he appeared particularly strong, particularly in his upper body.

His hands didn't appear to show any signs of injury, consistent with being used as a weapon. Likewise, his face, neck and exposed arms didn't appear to have any marks which might have indicated a violent struggle.

'Is there any reason you can think of why your wife has just suddenly vanished? Did you have an argument perhaps or was there anything troubling her that you're aware of?' asked Lewis.

'Look, I'll be perfectly honest with you mate. Since my accident I've been very difficult to live with. I know that myself and I try not to let my situation get me down, but it's very hard at times.

I get all moody and frustrated and I usually end up taking it out on Anne because she's the one who's always there, but I do love her, even though I'm not very good at showing it.'

Both men noticed the use of the present tense when Dean spoke of his wife. It seemed he was clinging to the hope she was still alive and would soon be found.

'We were both really looking forward to this cruise, probably for different reasons.

As you can imagine, day to day life for me can get very lonely and boring and being on a cruise always gives me a bit of a lift.

As far as Anne's concerned, she seems to be under an awful lot of pressure at work, much more than she used to, although she's been reluctant to take time off. I thought this was what we both needed and now this happens'.

During the interview, Dean was slumped forward in his wheelchair, a look of despair etched across his face.

'When you say she was under pressure at work, what exactly do you mean?' asked Lewis.

'Well, she's been there for over twenty years and has done really well for herself. It's a fairly small company and she started off as a junior, but now she's in charge of the company accounts.

I don't know if she's taken on too much or whatever, but she just seems to be permanently stressed out. She doesn't really discuss her work with me much and I suppose I've been too wrapped up in my own situation to give her enough support.'

'Do you think she's been under enough stress to have considered harming herself?'

'Not really. You wouldn't think so on the surface, but she's a really strong person mentally, she's had to be with what she's had to put up with since my accident.'

'Is she on any medication you're aware of?'

'She could be but I don't think so. She's certainly never mentioned any. I'm sure you'll understand, with my condition, there's so many pills in our bathroom it's hard to say.'

Lewis continued to probe, occasionally pausing to look at McIntyre, giving him the opportunity to interject.

In the past, as a Senior Investigating Officer, Lewis' role would have been confined to more of a general overview, but this was different. He didn't have a large team at his disposal and was acutely aware that he and McIntyre would have to rely on their own devices in this case.

After an hour or so with Dean, Lewis felt they'd extracted as much detail as they could from him up to that point.

He'd had a long, stressful day and was obviously completely shattered by the uncertainty of not knowing what had happened to his wife - or so it seemed. Lewis prepared to bring the conversation to an end.

'Is there anything else you think you can tell us that might help us find out what's happened to Anne?'

Dean looked forlornly at both men; a look of resignation etched across his tired features.

'You don't think she could have jumped, do you?'

It seemed more of an observation from Dean than a direct question.

'We certainly have to consider that as a possibility,' Lewis replied, 'but the security department have completed a thorough review of CCTV and it appears highly unlikely at this time.

One final question from me. Is there any area of the ship she has particularly frequented since you've been on board?'

Dean thought for a moment.

'Well, we've been round most of the ship, but she did go to the gym every day, sometimes more than once.

I don't know why, but in the past year she's become a bit of a gym fanatic. She goes at least three times a week at home. I think she uses it as a bit of stress relief to be honest.'

'We'll look into that, but I'm pretty sure it's already been checked out,' said Lewis, as McIntyre nodded in agreement.

'We'll speak again tomorrow Dean, but in the meantime try to get some rest. Be assured that we are doing everything possible to find Anne and we'll contact you as soon as we know anything.'

After arranging for the ship's nurse to ensure that Dean was being adequately cared for, both men then left.

It was late evening by the time McIntyre and Lewis returned to the incident room, where they prepared to update Konstantinos and Samaras with the details of Dean's interview.

Aware that he was an outsider and not part of the ship's crew, Lewis sat back, whilst McIntyre summarised the day's events.

'Mike and I have just spent some time with Anne's husband and I think we're both in agreement he doesn't appear likely to have been involved in her disappearance.

That said, we're not going to rule out the possibility at this stage, we may be proved wrong.

What has emerged from speaking to him, was that she appears to be a lady under a lot of stress. That of course leads to the possibility that she may have taken her own life, but unfortunately there is no evidence at the present time to support that.'

The others had little to add to the debrief, other than to confirm a thorough search of the ship had drawn a blank.

'What I'd like to do now,' continued McIntyre, 'is to have a good look through their stateroom. I feel certain there must be something there that will give us some idea as to why she has just disappeared.'

Lewis had a lecture to deliver at ten o'clock the following morning and still had some preparation to do, so it was agreed that McIntyre would conduct the search of the stateroom on his own, with assistance from the others if he required it.

McIntyre returned to the security control office to ensure every effort was being made by his staff to keep up the momentum of the search, particularly with regard to checking CCTV coverage.

He then made his way to the Ebsworth's stateroom on Deck 10. Before entering, he fixed a hi-viz *Do Not Enter* sticker to the stateroom door, even though the housekeeping department had already been warned that the room was to be left untouched until instructed otherwise.

McIntyre noticed the room was fairly untidy, but this was not uncommon in cruise ship cabins.

Being wheelchair friendly, the cabin was larger than normal but it was still fairly compact for two people and all their baggage. Despite the untidiness, there were no obvious signs of a struggle having taken place.

McIntyre knew that the room had already been searched earlier in the day, but only to confirm the absence of the missing person. His search would have to be more rigorous, more methodical. He was looking for something, anything, which might explain Anne's disappearance.

The first thing that struck him was that most of the clothing appeared to belong to Anne. He was no fashion expert, but McIntyre couldn't help noticing several pairs of shoes bearing the *Louboutin* and *Manolo Blahnik* labels, names which he recognised as being high end designers.

The rest of her clothing was a mixture of high street chic and designer labels, featuring Donna Karan, Chanel, Stella McCartney and Carolina Herrera. Even some of Dean's shoes and trainers were Louboutin and Blahnik.

Despite knowing nothing of their financial circumstances at that point, McIntyre was surprised at how expensive their clothing appeared to be.

It was now almost midnight and McIntyre knew a more detailed search of the stateroom would be better carried out in daylight. That way, any evidence of blood staining for example would be more easily detected, using the limited equipment at his disposal.

He took possession of a diary and a folder of documents which obviously belonged to Anne, which he intended to examine as a matter of urgency.

Before concluding the preliminary search, he stepped out on to the balcony. This was generously proportioned due to its position in a midships bulge. He switched off the lights in the stateroom behind him, so he could fully appreciate the darkness that closed in on him.

McIntyre leaned on the balcony rail and gazed straight ahead into the inky blackness.

They were now almost a third of the way across the Atlantic and the wind was gusting to force four or five. He shivered slightly but found the temperature to his liking after the stuffiness of the stateroom and the fact that he hadn't been outside on deck for over twenty-four hours.

Although they were cruising at no more than twenty-four knots, the white wake created by the ship seemed to race past far below him.

Stretching out maybe fifty metres from the side of the ship, illuminated by its many lights, he could see white flecks of spray spinning off the tops of the waves as they ploughed their way westwards.

He levelled his gaze towards the unseen horizon. There was no moon to cast light on the vast expanse of ocean beyond.

McIntyre glanced upwards. Despite the ship being ablaze with lights he could vaguely see a huge canopy of stars in the cloudless sky, which seemed to grow brighter as he accustomed his gaze.

He was struck by the absence of any other signs of ships' lights in the vicinity. They seemed to be all alone in the vastness of the ocean, although he knew the bridge radar screens would probably paint a different picture.

McIntyre found himself enjoying the bracing Atlantic wind and the almost tangible smell of the ocean and was reluctant to leave.

He pulled a chair up to the balcony rail and pondered the day's events. At this stage there appeared to no good reason for Anne's disappearance.

From what little he had gleaned up to that point, there was no evidence that she was still on board the ship. If that was the case, he thought, then the only other possibility was that, by whatever means, she had gone overboard.

McIntyre had been a ships security officer now for almost four years and he had experienced such an event once before, when a crew member had mysteriously disappeared.

It was subsequently confirmed that he had deliberately taken his own life. He also knew that around twenty people a year went missing from cruise ships, the majority being the result of an intentional or reckless act whilst at sea.

Understandably, the cruise lines themselves were very reluctant to publicise details of such occurrences and ships' crews tended not to talk too much about them.

As he gazed into the darkness, a mental picture flashed through his mind, almost like watching a film in slow-motion.

In it, he imagined Anne struggling alone in the hostile ocean. If she was still conscious at the time she entered the water, what was she feeling when she came to the surface?

He could visualise her blind panic as she desperately fought to stay afloat, watching the lights of the massive ship, which moments earlier had been her haven, disappearing into the distance.

Even if she managed to stay on the surface, survival would then become a matter of time.

Within one or two hours at most, she would gradually succumb to exhaustion, brought on by hypothermia and in all likelihood within a couple of hours after that, she would slowly sink to her watery grave.

McIntyre shuddered involuntarily, a combination of the

biting wind and his dark thoughts. He hoped he was wrong, but if she hadn't gone overboard, what was the alternative?

8

A few hours later, McIntyre was back in the security control room planning for the day ahead and catching up with details of any incidents which had occurred overnight. Fortunately, it had been quiet, which pleased him, given the additional responsibilities he now had to deal with.

His staff had continued reviewing footage of CCTV through-out the ship, starting with the time of Anne's disappearance and had come up with an interesting discovery.

At around half past eight on the night she was last seen, she had been positively identified in the ship's buffet restaurant on Deck 14. One of the restaurant supervisors had already been spoken to by security and had particularly remembered her, because of the fact that she was so well dressed.

Normally, on formal nights passengers tended to shun the buffet if they had gone to the trouble of dressing up and preferred to use the more formal dining rooms.

Closer examination of the images from the buffet had revealed a more intriguing development however. Anne appeared to be in company with a male, who quite obviously wasn't her husband.

This in itself may not normally have assumed great significance, as passengers tended to interact more easily with strangers in the informal setting of the buffet restaurant. To McIntyre however, it looked as though the two were more than passing acquaintances.

Finding this male had now become a matter of priority, but in a ship with nearly three thousand passengers, it might be no easy task.

Whilst waiting for Lewis to finish delivering his morning lecture in the ship's theatre, McIntyre made his way to the incident room.

He decided to use the time productively, by starting to look through the diary and correspondence he had taken from the Ebsworth's stateroom the previous evening.

After sifting through the paperwork for a short time, he came upon the cruise invoice for the Ebsworth booking. Clearly, Anne had dealt with all aspects of the booking personally, as the invoice was in her name.

McIntyre felt a surge of adrenalin as he read it however. Anne and Dean Ebsworth were not the only passengers listed on the invoice. She had booked and paid for a total of four passengers.

In addition to herself and Dean, the names Lee Andrews and Craig Leonard were shown on the invoice.

During the earlier interview with Dean, no mention had been made of anyone else travelling in their party. Had he omitted to mention it for reasons which he didn't want to disclose, or did he simply not know?

McIntyre now had a positive line of enquiry to pursue but first he needed to speak to Dean again.

He made his way down to Deck 5 where he entered the ship's theatre at the top level.

Located at the bow of the ship, the theatre was as big as

many London West End venues and spanned the height of three decks, from stage level to balcony. With seating for over a thousand passengers it was an impressive auditorium.

Today it was almost half full, indicating the popularity of the speaker, or at least his subject matter.

On stage below him, he could make out the unmistakeable figure of Mike Lewis, resplendent in white tuxedo, red bow tie and red carnation buttonhole.

McIntyre smiled inwardly at the sight of his former colleague, whom he was used to seeing in less flamboyant attire and vowed to tease him mercilessly at the earliest opportunity.

Lewis paced confidently along the front of the stage, his voice clear and authoritative over his wireless, head-worn microphone.

Guest speakers were not permitted to use notes to deliver their presentations and the only prompts allowed were those available on the PowerPoint note capability.

McIntyre waited whilst Lewis finished his presentation and invited questions from the audience. Three or four hands went up before Lewis took the first question.

McIntyre guessed that it would be at least another fifteen minutes before his friend could leave the theatre without appearing abrupt, so he made his way to his favourite speciality coffee bar, where he texted Lewis to join him as soon as he was free.

After about twenty minutes, Lewis arrived and eagerly accepted the americano McIntyre had already ordered and which was quickly brought over by one of the ever-attentive waiters.

'Sorry I took so long,' Lewis apologised, 'but you always

get one who tries to trip you up with an awkward question at the end.'

'You'll be interested to know', said McIntyre, 'that there have been some significant developments since we last spoke.'

Having been brought up to speed with events, Lewis returned to his cabin to change out of his 'stage' clothes and agreed to reconvene in the incident room as quickly as possible.

A few minutes later they were joined there by Captain Alex, who had been alerted there had been an apparent breakthrough in the investigation. McIntyre addressed the captain directly.

'We still have no idea what may have happened to Anne, but we should now be in a position to move things forward quickly.'

McIntyre sensed Captain Alex was still wrestling with the possibility that Anne may have been lost overboard and seemed keen to ensure they had done everything they possibly could to exclude that scenario.

He knew the captain's decision not to turn the ship around when he first heard that the passenger had gone missing, lay at the heart of his dilemma.

McIntyre brought Captain Alex up to date with the details of the two new passengers of interest and assured him they would be traced and interviewed without delay.

As soon as the captain had left, Lewis and McIntyre made their way to Dean Ebsworth's stateroom.

After knocking and getting no reply, McIntyre entered using the master card that all members of security carried. This allowed them to gain entry to any of the nearly 1500 cabins (or staterooms as the guest cabins were called) throughout the ship, although they were only expected to use them in case of emergency.

Dean was nowhere to be seen, nor was there any sign of his wheelchair. As they were leaving, they were met by the room steward who told them Dean had said he was going down to the casino.

They made their way back down to the casino area on Deck 5, where to their relief, they found Dean engrossed in the slot machines. Both were surprised to see him out of his stateroom, given the situation he currently found himself in, but guessed he needed the distraction.

'There's something we need to talk to you about,' McIntyre began. 'Let's go somewhere a bit more private where we can have a chat.'

Rather than return to Dean's stateroom, the trio moved to a secluded alcove outside one of the speciality restaurants on Deck 5.

'Have you found her?' Dean asked, a look of anticipation flitting across his tired features.

'Afraid not,' McIntyre replied. 'I hope you don't mind, but I've been going through some of the paperwork we found in your stateroom and we came across the invoice for your cruise. Would I be right in thinking most of the arrangements were done by Anne?'

'Yeah, she dealt with everything. She takes care of all our correspondence at home. I just let her get on with it,' Dean replied.

'Who are the other two people shown on the invoice?' continued McIntyre, deliberately excluding gender or names. Dean looked at both men with a look of genuine astonishment.

'What do you mean two other people? I don't understand. There's just the two of us. You must be mistaken,' Dean almost stammered.

McIntyre saw no point in withholding the evidence from Dean at this stage, so he presented him with the invoice. Dean examined it closely, in silence at first, then his hands began to tremble. Either he was a very good actor, or this had come as a complete shock to him.

'I just can't believe what you've just shown me. I'm sure there must be some innocent explanation,' gasped Dean, visibly shocked.

'Obviously we're going to confirm the details with the purser's office, but I thought I'd give you the opportunity first to tell us anything you know about the other two passengers. However, you're saying you know nothing about them, is that right?' asked McIntyre.

Dean nodded. At that point, McIntyre decided not to mention the sighting of Anne with the unknown male in the buffet restaurant on the night of her disappearance. His first priority was to identify this person, before pursuing it further with Dean.

'Christ, I need a drink, I'm struggling to take in what you've just told me,' Dean muttered.

McIntyre wasn't particularly keen on having Dean wandering the ship alone in his wheelchair, drinking alcohol, particularly given the news he had just received, but he knew that as a paying passenger, he was powerless to stop him. A quick call to the security office however, would ensure that his colleagues kept a close eye on him. Only if Dean became a danger to himself or others, would they intervene.

The next stop for McIntyre and Lewis was the purser's office, centrally located on Deck 4. They needed to confirm the details on the Ebsworth invoice were correct and no mistake had been made.

It came as no surprise to discover the information held on the passenger manifest matched exactly that on the invoice and payment for all four passengers shown, had indeed been made by Anne Ebsworth.

They then made their way back down to the security control room. Having gleaned the names of the other two passengers on the invoice, McIntyre knew it would be a simple task to retrieve their photographs from the ship's security system.

Before doing so, he brought up the best image taken of Anne and the mystery male in the buffet restaurant on the night of her disappearance. With this image frozen on one of the security monitors, McIntyre then logged into the passenger list, which displayed a photograph of each passenger, taken just prior to embarkation.

Both men felt a sense of nervous anticipation as McIntyre typed in the first name - *Lee Andrews*.

As the image flashed up on screen, two pairs of eyes simultaneously glanced up at the still image from the buffet. They looked at each other fleetingly and shook their heads.

Craig Leonard was the next name typed into the system. Almost immediately, the investigators could tell the images on both screens were identical. Both knew they could now begin to make some headway in their investigation.

Back in the incident room, McIntyre and Lewis were once more joined by Konstantinos and Samaras. By now the latter two were perfectly happy to step away from the investigation, particularly since progress was apparently being made.

McIntyre had not yet been able to conduct a full daylight search of the Ebsworth stateroom and enlisted their help in securing the room properly, by having the master entry facility disabled. Despite the warning stickers on the stateroom door, he did not fully trust the housekeeping staff to keep away from the room.

The next step was to trace and interview Andrews and Leonard.

The investigators already knew their stateroom numbers from the invoice and the records held in the purser's office. What intrigued McIntyre most however, was the different standard of the staterooms.

Lee Andrews stateroom was on Deck 3, room 3144, which was located on the starboard side of the ship, very near to the bow. It was also an inside cabin which meant there was no sea view. From his intimate knowledge of the ship, he knew this was one of the cheapest and least comfortable passenger cabins on the entire vessel.

By comparison, Craig Leonard's stateroom was located on Deck 6, room 6201, port side. This stateroom had a balcony, albeit with an obstructed view and was positioned between midships and the stern.

The disparity between the position and quality of the staterooms was very evident. It was almost as if the occupants had deliberately been placed as far apart as possible and in differing degrees of comfort.

It was time to find out why.

9

Certain basic information is required before a cruise ship passenger is permitted to embark. Details include; full name, date of birth, nationality, home address, passport number with date and place of issue and details of emergency contacts.

In addition, passengers travelling to the United States from certain countries, including the United Kingdom, are required to be in possession of a visa waiver called an ESTA (Electronic System for Travel Authorization). The application form for an ESTA requires the applicant to include all of the above, but additionally requests parents' details, employment information and details of previous criminal history.

As the Enterprise Endeavour was a US registered ship, travelling to a port of entry in the United States, all of these details would be forwarded by the cruise line for screening by the US Department of Homeland Security.

In his role as chief security officer, McIntyre was aware of this and knew that, should he require to access it, he would be able to view a considerable amount of detail about the two passengers he now proposed to interview.

A decision now had to be made as to which of the two passengers was to be interviewed first. Logic dictated that it should be Craig Leonard, as the last verified sighting of Anne on the ship had been in his company. The investigators returned to the purser's office to unearth as much detail as they could about him, from the details supplied at the time of booking and from his ESTA application.

They discovered that Leonard was forty-three years old and was born in London. He currently lived in a small town in Kent, which was only about ten miles from where the Ebsworth's lived. His emergency contact was shown as a brother, who lived in London. Leonard was the holder of a British passport.

In his ESTA application he had declared that both parents were deceased. He had given details of a minor assault conviction some years previously and gave his current occupation as personal trainer and fitness coach.

Armed with this information, McIntyre and Lewis set about drawing up an interview plan. Both men agreed that the initial interview would be very brief, as the primary objective was to discover what had happened to Anne and if possible, to facilitate her safe return.

By now it was early afternoon on the second full day since Anne had disappeared.

McIntyre and Lewis made their way to Leonard's stateroom but were not surprised to find that he wasn't there. They spoke to his room steward who was unable to assist with his current whereabouts. However, the steward was able to tell the investigators that although Leonard was the sole occupant of the stateroom, he had been frequently visited there by a 'lady' whom the steward quickly identified as Anne Ebsworth, from the photograph which McIntyre showed him.

It was now a question of finding Leonard, who at that precise moment could be anywhere on the ship. The most obvious way was to ring his mobile phone, which McIntyre did, but it went unanswered.

The investigators split up, with McIntyre setting out to check if Leonard had made a booking for that evening at any of the onboard restaurants, whilst Lewis was delegated to visit the ship's gym, which both men felt was a likely venue for him to be using, given his stated occupation.

Within minutes, Lewis was in contact to let his colleague know that Leonard was indeed at that location

McIntyre quickly made his way to the gym, which was located within the spa area at the bow of the ship, on Deck 12. Although fairly small, the gym was packed with state-of-the-art equipment, including cross trainers, rowing machines, exercise bikes, multi gym machines and a section for free standing weights. Floor to ceiling windows gave an uninterrupted view of the open ocean beyond.

Lewis met him at the entrance and discreetly pointed out Leonard, who was doing bicep curls in the weights section. Whilst Lewis had been observing him for several minutes, this was McIntyre's first sight of their quarry and he was immediately impressed with his well-honed physique.

At a quick glance, he estimated that Leonard was at least six feet tall and probably weighed around two hundred and ten pounds. His shaven head gave him a somewhat menacing appearance. He was wearing thigh length training shorts and a matching sleeveless vest which were both functional and designed to show off his toned body to best advantage.

Leonard finished his bicep curls and walked towards the water fountain at the edge of the gym, where he took a long swig, before mopping the perspiration from his face and neck with his towel. He looked quite flushed and McIntyre rightly guessed he had come to the end of his session, as he dropped the used towel into the laundry receptacle and headed slowly towards the exit.

It was almost certain that Leonard would now want to shower and change, but would he return to his stateroom to do so or use the facilities in the men's changing room located just outside the gym? McIntyre could see that he wasn't carrying anything with him and guessed that his belongings would be in the changing room. As he had anticipated, Leonard headed straight there.

McIntyre motioned for Lewis to stay behind and casually entered the changing room behind him. Although McIntyre was in uniform Leonard barely glanced up at him. This didn't surprise McIntyre, who knew one of the golden rules of surveillance - hide in plain sight, be seen but not noticed.

Leonard opened one of the combination lockers and retrieved his clothing and other belongings. He grabbed a freshly laundered towel from a pile in one corner and began to undress.

McIntyre guessed at this point that Leonard was about to take a shower but was concerned that he may also want to use the sauna which was located next to the shower cubicles. If he did so, it was likely they could be here for at least the next half hour, which McIntyre was keen to avoid, as he was now anxious to speak to Leonard without further delay. He was relieved when he saw Leonard head straight for one of the shower cubicles.

McIntyre briefly left the changing room to contact the security control room, to request that a couple of extra officers be sent up, as he had no way of knowing how Leonard would react when eventually confronted.

He re-entered the changing room and made his way to a locked door bearing the sign *crew only* which led directly into the gym office. Leaving the door slightly ajar, he could just make out the shower cubicles and the entrance to the sauna without being seen himself.

After about five minutes, Leonard left the shower, completed drying himself off and headed back towards his locker. McIntyre then locked the crew entrance door and made his way back through the gym to the changing room entrance, unseen by Leonard.

By now the two additional security officers were discreetly positioned behind the spa reception desk nearby, whilst McIntyre and Lewis waited for Leonard to come out.

As soon as Leonard exited the changing room, McIntyre stepped forward, blocking his path. Lewis stood several paces behind him, whilst the two uniformed security officers remained where they were, only feet away, sufficiently close to respond instantly, should Leonard react violently.

'Good afternoon sir. My name is Calum McIntyre and I'm the chief security officer on the ship. I wonder if it would be possible to speak to you somewhere in private for a few minutes? There's an issue which has arisen that I hope you may be able to help me with.'

McIntyre's initial approach was deliberately vague and non-confrontational. Removing Leonard from the scene with the minimum of fuss was his main priority. Leonard gave no indication he had seen McIntyre just a few minutes previously in the changing room.

'Sure, what's it about?' said Leonard, his face expressionless.

If he was concerned, nothing in his demeanour gave it away. McIntyre was used to making instant judgments on individuals who were suddenly placed in a fight or flight situation, but he felt sure Leonard posed no immediate threat.

'If it's ok with you, we'll jump in a lift and go down to my office where I'll explain everything. Happy with that? Oh, and by the way, this gentleman here is a colleague of mine, Mike Lewis. I'll explain his role when we get downstairs.'

The trio then started to make their way to one of the service lifts. As they moved off, McIntyre motioned silently to the two security officers to make their way one deck down via the stairway, to join them in the lift.

Although he felt confident Leonard was compliant, he was still the last person to be seen in the presence of the missing passenger and McIntyre didn't want to take any chances.

Having taken their time walking to the lift on Deck 12, it appeared perfectly natural when it stopped on Deck 11 and the two security officers sauntered in, feigning indifference and completely ignoring them.

On reaching Deck zero, the two officers peeled off in one direction, whilst McIntyre, Lewis and Leonard headed for the security office. The choice of venue for the interview was deliberate. Here they were in the crew area of the ship and in a more secure environment.

On reaching the security complex, McIntyre ushered Leonard into a small interview room located next to his office. The only fixtures in this room were a small table and four chairs. It was cramped and slightly claustrophobic, which McIntyre knew could give him an advantage in a situation where he didn't want the interviewee to feel too comfortable, whilst at the same time not being overly oppressive.

He motioned for Leonard to sit at the side of the table furthest from the door, whilst he and Lewis took up position opposite him. Leonard still appeared fairly unperturbed at the situation he had suddenly found himself in, but McIntyre noticed he frequently licked his lips as if his mouth was dry.

Once everyone was seated, McIntyre deliberately waited for about twenty seconds before speaking. He wanted to ramp up the tension without it appearing obvious he was doing so. Still, Leonard didn't noticeably react.

'Right, once again thanks for agreeing to come with us.' McIntyre began. 'I've already introduced both of us upstairs. As I told you, I'm the chief security officer here on the Enterprise Endeavour, so I'm one of the ship's officers. My colleague, Mike Lewis is not actually a crew member, but he is on the ship in an official capacity as a guest speaker.

He and I previously served together in the police and he's here today to assist me, with the full knowledge and permission of the captain. Before we go any further, can I just confirm that you are Craig Leonard and your stateroom number is 6201?'

'Spot on,' replied Leonard casually, maintaining his previous air of apparent indifference. McIntyre effected another long pause before continuing.

'I'll come straight to the point, Craig. The reason why we think you might be able to help us is because one of the ship's passengers has been missing for almost two days now. A lady by the name of Anne Ebsworth. We believe you might know her. Would that be correct?'

Leonard remained impassive, but his Adam's apple began to quiver, a sure sign of nervous tension.

'Look, am I a suspect or something? You're both ex cops and I've had a little spot of bother with the law in the past. Aren't you supposed to caution me and all that sort of thing? I notice your mate's taking notes, so it feels like I could be stitched up here.'

McIntyre knew instantly from Leonard's reply that he had a challenge on his hands. He had agreed beforehand with Lewis that he would conduct the interview, whilst Lewis kept a contemporaneous written record of what was said.

They had also discussed the practicalities of issuing a caution prior to any interview commencing, but had ruled it out for several reasons.

Firstly, they were in international waters and therefore outside the jurisdiction of any law enforcement agency. Secondly, there was no evidence at this stage a crime had been committed and lastly neither investigator was currently an accredited law enforcement officer and therefore not bound by the normal rules of evidence. If the situation changed at all, then McIntyre fully intended to issue a caution, even though not legally obliged to do so, but that time had not yet come.

'Craig, we're not accusing you of anything, but we're dealing with a missing person who hasn't been seen on board for almost forty-eight hours now and that to me is very concerning. All we're asking for at this point is your help in finding out what could have happened to her or where we may find her if she's still on the ship,' continued McIntyre. 'Now I'll ask you again, do you know Anne Ebsworth?'

Leonard paused for several seconds before replying.

'You know if I wanted to, I could just make no comment to all your questions and get up and walk out of here.'

'You're absolutely right of course,' McIntyre went on 'but I really don't think that would be a good idea, Craig. If you refuse to answer my questions, I think I would be entitled to draw an inference that you had something to hide. I would then have to bring the matter to the attention of the captain. He has absolute authority on this ship and I think he would probably issue an instruction that you were to be confined to your stateroom until this matter is sorted out. I'm sure none of us want that to happen, do we?'

McIntyre felt confident that Leonard wouldn't follow through with his implied threat of non-cooperation. He knew that interviewing witnesses or suspects, particularly the latter, could be like a game of poker at times, with neither party willing to show its hand. He also suspected that Leonard was trying to turn the tables on him, by getting McIntyre to reveal what *he* knew, rather than answering the questions himself.

He guessed Leonard had probably been in trouble with the police more often than he had just mentioned and which he had declared on his ESTA application. As far as McIntyre was concerned, Leonard had issued a challenge – if you want some information from me, you're going to have to work for it.

'What do you want me to tell you?' Leonard replied.

He was leaning back in his chair, arms folded tightly across his chest, a classic defensive posture. McIntyre noticed his right leg was constantly vibrating under the table. Despite his efforts to appear in control, McIntyre knew Leonard was beginning to exhibit unmistakeable signs of stress.

'Just tell us what your relationship is with Anne Ebsworth

for starters? To avoid beating about the bush, we know that she booked you on this cruise and also paid for it. You must realise it hasn't exactly been difficult for us to find that out.'

'Pointless denying it then,' Leonard replied morosely.

McIntyre had now asked him on three separate occasions to confirm that he knew Anne Ebsworth, but so far Leonard's non-committal response was as far as they had got. He glanced at his colleague Lewis and both men instinctively knew the next move. Without a word being spoken, Lewis slid his notepad across the desk to McIntyre.

It was now time for the good cop, bad cop routine. Lewis fixed Leonard with a disarming smile.

'Good, we're beginning to get somewhere,' he soothed, giving Leonard the impression he had so far been nothing but co-operative, which of course he hadn't.

'Now obviously we're very concerned about Anne and I imagine you are too, so let's just start at the beginning, shall we? First of all, how long have you known her?'

'Just over a year.'

The tactic of changing interviewer seemed to have worked instantly, even though Leonard probably realised exactly what was happening. Very rarely did it fail.

'Good, and how did you two meet up?' continued Lewis.

'She started coming to the gym where I work and asked if I could draw up a fitness plan for her. That's what I did, then after a while she asked if she could use me as her personal trainer. I have quite a few clients who I do that for and as she seemed to have the money, I was more than happy to oblige.'

'Right, I'm getting the picture,' Lewis went on. 'Sorry if it seems like I'm prying, but in your experience is it usual for a client to reward their personal trainer with an all-expenses paid cruise?'

'Well, it's certainly never happened to me before, but some clients can be quite generous in different ways, depending on how well off they are.'

'Would you describe Anne as well off?' asked Lewis 'I mean do you know what she does for a living?'

'She doesn't talk about her work much, but I think she's involved with some sort of engineering company, might even be a director and she never appears to be short of cash. She has a couple of cars, one of them quite expensive and she seems to go on cruises fairly regularly, so I'm guessing she's fairly minted.'

'Did you know Anne was married?' Lewis continued. It was time to up the tempo. Leonard seemed momentarily taken aback by the directness of the question. His posture stiffened.

'Not for a while, but obviously I do now,' he responded, somewhat ambiguously.

'We're all men together here,' Lewis continued, trying to appear more conversational than inquisitorial.

'I presume the two of you have become more than just good friends?'

'Well yeah, there's no point denying it.'

Leonard was now beginning to give them what they wanted to hear.

'What about her husband? Is he aware of your existence? Does he know you're on board?'

'I presume you know he's in a wheelchair?' Leonard answered. 'As far as I'm aware, he doesn't know anything about the two of us and from what Anne's told me, I'm not sure if he'd be that bothered.'

'When was the last time you saw her?'

Lewis already knew the time that they had last been seen together, but Leonard's answer would establish to what extent he was telling them the truth.

'A couple of nights ago. She texted me to meet her in the buffet up on Deck 14. I think it was around eight o'clock. We ate together. Normally she went to the main dining room with her old man, but she said he wasn't feeling too good, so obviously it was a chance for us to be together.'

'And how long were you in each other's company?'

'Probably a couple of hours tops,' Leonard replied. 'After we'd eaten, we went down to one of the bars on Deck 5 and had a drink or two. She'd got all dressed up 'cos I seem to remember it was one of the formal nights and I think she just wanted to be seen. I hadn't bothered, so to be honest I felt a bit under dressed alongside her.

After a couple of hours, she said she was going back to their cabin to check on her old man and we agreed to meet up the next day, but I haven't heard from her since. She hasn't even replied to any of my texts and she hasn't been going to the gym, which I'm very surprised about.'

'Don't you think that's strange?' Lewis continued 'We know that you've been seeing her every day since you've been on board. Why the sudden silence do you think?'

'That's what I don't understand myself. I'm guessing maybe her old man isn't too well but I haven't seen her in the gym or anywhere around the ship and it's strange that she's not been in touch. In fact, I'm a bit annoyed about it.'

Lewis glanced at McIntyre who spread his palms outwards

to silently indicate they had taken the interview as far as they could at that stage.

'Right Craig. Obviously, we may have to speak to you again if we can't trace Anne in the meantime,' Lewis concluded. 'One last thing. Do you mind if we come with you to have a quick look round your cabin, just to satisfy ourselves that she's not there?'

'No problem,' Leonard said, seemingly visibly relieved that the interview was over.

As they left the cramped confines of the interview room to make their way to Leonard's stateroom, Lewis couldn't help noticing the difference between the crew and passenger areas of the ship.

He had never ventured 'below decks' before on any of the cruises he had lectured on, even though some of the cabins he had occupied had been perilously close. It was almost like being on two different ships. Gone was the glitz and glamour to be seen in the passenger section. Vibrant colour was replaced by plain walls, painted either in beige or grey.

Functionality was the order of the day and Lewis was reminded of images of naval vessels he had seen on TV and films. He shuddered to think that for some of the crew, this was all they would see for literally months on end. Although he already knew it, he realised at that point, the life of a cruise ship crew member was far from glamorous.

Leonard inserted his sea pass into the door entry slot and they all moved inside his stateroom. It was reasonably spacious, particularly for a single occupant. A double bed dominated the centre of the room, with a small bedside table on either side. The standard fridge and mini combination safe were concealed within a small cabinet along one wall. A wall-mounted TV, which was switched on and tuned to the bridge cam, was located above the cabinet.

Running parallel to one side of the bed was a small settee with a coffee table in front of it. The en-suite bathroom contained the usual shower-toilet-sink combination. A floor- to- ceiling sliding glass door led out on to a small balcony.

Looking straight ahead from the balcony, there was an unobstructed view of the ocean beyond, but looking over the balcony rail, the only view was that of the top of a long line of orange lifeboats, hung on gantries by the side of the ship.

He wasn't sure why, but McIntyre had expected the room to be untidy. To his surprise it was the exact opposite. As the investigators moved through the accommodation with prac-tised efficiency, they noted there was no clutter in the room or the en-suite whatsoever.

All Leonard's clothing was neatly hung or folded in the ward-robe and his toiletries carefully arranged on the glass shelves in the small wall cabinet next to the sink. To McIntyre the room was almost too tidy. Was Leonard always this fastidious, or had efforts been made to tidy up the cabin for some reason?

'Are you always this organised, Craig?' ventured McIntyre, testing his reaction.

'Force of habit mate. I spent almost twenty years in the Army. They don't encourage slovenliness, especially in the Para's.'

This was an interesting and unexpected revelation, which would require further investigation, but it could certainly explain the state of the room and allay any immediate suspicions the inves-tigators may have had, that it had been sanitised.

Nothing in Leonard's room gave any indication of a recent disturbance. His initial interview had confirmed his relationship with Anne Ebsworth, but had given no indication as to what may have happened to her. If Leonard was to be believed, her current whereabouts were as much a mystery to him as to anyone else.

What troubled the investigators however, when they sat down to plan their next move, was Leonard's noticeable lack of concern. The only emotion he had shown during the interview was apparent annoyance she hadn't been in touch since their last meeting. For the time being however, it was time to move on. They now had to locate and speak to Lee Andrews.

10

Returning to the purser's office, McIntyre accessed Lee Andrews' details. At twenty-eight years of age, he was considerably younger than the rest of the party. According to the address given, he lived in the same town as the Ebsworth's. The holder of a UK passport, he had declared his next of kin as his mother, who appeared to live at the same address. On his ESTA application, he had stated he was self-employed, but had not given an occupation. Under previous criminal history, he had merely declared *minor driving offences*.

'Not a lot to go on there,' Lewis sighed. 'Wouldn't surprise me if there was a bit more in the way of criminal convictions though. They usually start off by admitting driving offences, but not the more serious stuff.'

'I was thinking exactly the same thing,' agreed McIntyre.

It was now late evening, but both men knew that they needed to speak to Andrews before calling it a day. Leonard's presence on board had been partly explained, but Andrews remained a mystery.

McIntyre retrieved a mobile phone number from Andrews' embarkation details.

'Let's try the easy way first,' he said, before dialling up the number. After a few rings, a male voice answered.

'Yeah, who is it?'

'Lee?' A long, silent pause ensued.

'Is that Lee Andrews?' McIntyre continued.

In the background he could hear a lot of noise, as if the person answering was in one of the public areas of the ship, probably one of the bars, he thought.

'Who wants to know?' came the wary reply.

'Lee, I'm Calum McIntyre. I'm the ship's security officer. There's something I need to speak to you about.'

'You need to speak to me? Why, what's the problem?'

'Well, hopefully there isn't a problem, but I still need to speak to you urgently,' McIntyre replied.

'Go ahead then, but I hope it won't take long because I'm a bit busy at the moment.'

'Look Lee, this isn't something that can be done over the phone. We'll have to meet up to sort this out, face to face.'

'Ok. Can I come and see you first thing tomorrow? Like I said it's not very convenient at the moment. At the end of the day, I'm not exactly going to disappear off the ship, am I?' McIntyre detected a note of sarcasm in this reply.

Although he hadn't confirmed his identity, McIntyre was confident that he was speaking to Andrews.

'Hopefully this won't take long. Tell you what Lee, I'll meet you outside your cabin in fifteen minutes. I know which one you're in.'

McIntyre then terminated the call before giving Andrews the chance to accept or decline his invitation.

McIntyre glanced across at Lewis.

'Seems like he wasn't too keen on speaking to me straight away. I wonder why? You heard me say I'd meet him outside his cabin in fifteen, but let's get over there now. If there's anything there he doesn't want us to see, he'll go back straight away and we'll have the element of surprise if we're waiting for him.'

Both men immediately made their way to Deck 3 which was located slightly above the waterline. Not that it made much difference in Andrews' case, as his inside cabin precluded any view of the sea, but McIntyre knew it made a big difference in terms of the motion of the ship.

As they reached room 3144, which was allocated to Andrews, McIntyre knocked loudly on the door. As expected, he got no response. The time between McIntyre terminating the phone conversation and them getting there had been less than three minutes. They found a recess nearby where they could observe the corridor leading to Andrews' cabin without being seen and waited.

A couple of minutes later they saw the slightly built figure of a young male almost running towards them. He stopped outside 3144 and looked all around him. He seemed nervous and slightly out of breath. It was obvious he had got there in a rush. As he was about to open the door using his sea pass, both men stepped from the recess. The male jumped back a step, a startled expression flitting across his face.

'Hello Lee, Calum McIntyre, chief security officer. We spoke a few minutes ago. Nice of you to make it so quickly. Been in the wars I see.'

'I was just going to get something from my cabin. If you give me a couple of seconds, I'll come back and join you,' the young man blustered.

'As a matter of fact, Lee, we need to have a look inside your cabin anyway, so we might as well do that now whilst we're here and I'll tell you what this is all about.'

McIntyre's tone was firm and just to emphasise the issue was not up for debate, he opened the cabin door using his master pass and ushered Andrews inside.

Unlike Leonard's room, this one was extremely untidy. Lewis in particular wasn't surprised, as it was the smallest passenger cabin he had ever seen on any cruise ship. A single bed extended almost the entire length of one wall. At the end of the bed was a small desk with a small screen TV located on the wall above it. A compact wardrobe was fixed to the wall opposite the bed and in the bottom corner of the room was a tiny en-suite bathroom. Anyone sitting on the toilet would almost be in the shower cubicle, which was only just large enough for an average sized person to turn around in.

In McIntyre's experience even some crew members had better accommodation. Whatever the reason for Andrews being on this cruise, comfort had not been a consideration when his booking had been made.

As soon as he entered the room, Andrews quickly folded back the duvet and almost hid it under his pillow. He sat down on the bed with his back pressed tightly against the pillow. It seemed there was something he didn't want his visitors to see.

'What's this all about? Are you allowed to just barge in here without my permission?' Andrews exclaimed a little tetchily.

He was now beginning to recover his composure and giving out signals that he may have found himself in trouble before, other than for his previously declared minor motoring offences.

McIntyre perched himself on the opposite end of the bed, whilst Lewis drew up the small chair located next to the desk and sat down. With three of them in the room, the place felt crowded.

As soon as they had set eyes on Andrews for the first time, they noticed that he had very obvious facial injuries. There was a fairly deep cut about half an inch long on the bridge of his nose. He also had what appeared to be the classic symptoms of a black eye around his right eye. The area around this eye was a livid, dark blue and violet colour, consistent with a violent event having happened within the last couple of days.

From their experience, both investigators knew if this injury was any older, the bruising would have turned a yellowish, green colour by that stage. There also appeared to be a laceration to his lower lip, which appeared slightly swollen. For this reason alone, Andrews had now become a person of extreme interest.

After introducing Lewis, McIntyre carried on with the conversation.

'The reason we're here Lee, is because one of our passengers is missing. Anne Ebsworth. We understand you know her, right?'

'What makes you think that?' Andrews responded, by now beginning to sound more confident, a little cocky, even.

'I don't think it, I know it,' McIntyre went on forcefully, keen to avoid a prolonged and unnecessary bout of verbal sparring. 'She made the booking for you and she appears to have paid for it. All very easy for us to check up on. You also live in the same town, so I'm sure it's not just a coincidence you've ended up on the same cruise together.'

Andrews remained silent for a short while, but both men could sense that he was frantically trying to figure out his response. A sheen of sweat was becoming visible on his forehead, accentuated by his gaunt, pasty features.

'Ok, I used to work at the same place as her, Ace Valves. We've sort of kept in touch. The last time I spoke to her she told me her and Dean, that's her old man, were coming on this cruise. I've never been on a cruise before. In fact, I've never even been abroad before and told her I wished I could afford it. She said if I wanted to she could book me on their cruise and I could pay her back when I was able to.'

'Sounds very generous of her. You must be very good friends?' remarked McIntyre.

'We get along pretty well.'

'I mentioned earlier you seem to have been in the wars. What happened to your face?'

'I fell down some stairs.'

'Oh really?' McIntyre said, feigning concern. 'I hope you've reported it. We really need to know about any incidents involving passengers. Especially slips and trips and that sort of thing, just to make sure there's no hazards around the ship which we're not aware of.'

'It was all down to me really. I had a bit too much to drink a couple of nights back and I misjudged one of the steps on the way back to my cabin. It wasn't anybody's fault but my own, so I don't want any fuss.'

'Were you knocked out at all?'

'No, I got up right away and came straight back to my cabin. I was more embarrassed than anything else, but fortunately I don't think there was anyone around to see me.'

'Can you remember exactly which flight of steps you fell down?' McIntyre enquired, hoping that CCTV footage might help to confirm Andrews' explanation.

'No. it was somewhere between the deck where most of the bars are and this one.'

'Do you think you should get checked over just as a precaution? That nose of yours looks like it could do with a few steri-strips to close up the cut a bit.'

McIntyre was thinking ahead. If he could get Andrews' injuries independently documented by a doctor or nurse from the ship's sick bay, it may be good evidence later, should it be required.

'Somebody told me it costs a fortune to see a doctor on a cruise ship,' Andrews replied.

'Don't worry about that. I'll sort it out for you. All part of the service,' said McIntyre disarmingly. 'Now to get back to the reason why we're here. As I've already told you, Anne has been reported missing. When was the last time you saw her?'

'I've only seen her twice since we left Southampton. The first time was on Sunday, about three hours after we got on board. Then I saw her again the following afternoon, round about four o'clock I think, up near the pool bar. Haven't see her since.'

'Don't you think that's a bit strange?'

'Not really. Look, this sounds a bit odd, but she didn't really want Dean to know that she'd paid for me to come along. I think he's a bit of a control freak and probably wouldn't approve. The agreement was that I would do my own thing and to be honest, that suits me down to the ground.'

'I know this is a pretty big ship, but what would happen if you bumped into Dean somewhere on board?' probed McIntyre.

'I've seen him around town. He's hard to miss, especially

being in a wheelchair, but he's never met me, so he's no idea what I look like.'

'Apart from Anne, Dean and yourself, is there anyone else in your party?'

McIntyre studied Andrews' face intently as he posed the question. The young man struggled to hold his gaze.

'Not that I know of. I'm not sure what you're on about.'

'Just checking, that's all,' McIntyre responded casually. 'Because Anne's missing, we need to track down everybody on board who might know her.'

He wasn't convinced that Andrews was telling the truth on this point, but he had manoeuvred him into giving an answer.

'Last thing for the time being Lee. As we've now confirmed that you and Anne know each other and the fact she's still missing, we need to be one hundred per cent sure she's not in your cabin. It's pretty cosy in here but could you just lift up the mattress for a moment so we can have a quick look under the bed?'

McIntyre could easily have knelt down to look under the bed himself, but he needed Andrews to move away from the duvet.

'You're joking aren't you? There's hardly enough room for my bag under that bed.'

Andrews remained firmly seated at the head of the bed.

'Only take a second Lee, up you get,' McIntyre said, motioning upwards with both palms raised, indicating that refusal was not an option.

Andrews reluctantly stood up, but kept his left hand firmly pressed down on the folded duvet.

Without further ado, McIntyre grabbed the outside edge of the mattress with both hands and yanked it firmly upwards and away from him, towards the wall. The only item visible under the metal bedframe was a large rucksack.

'Ok, thanks for that,' said McIntyre, in a matter-of-fact tone, as he returned the mattress to its original position. 'I'll just leave the bed tidy for you, shall I?'

Before Andrews could react, McIntyre grabbed the duvet and spread it out to its original position, covering the bed. Andrews flung himself down on the bed, but he was too late.

11

'Stand up Lee,' commanded McIntyre firmly. Lewis, who had remained seated by the desk up to this point, was also quickly on his feet and moved in closer. He too had noticed Andrews grab for the duvet when they first entered the room and what he now saw before him came as no surprise.

Andrews, realising that the game was up, reluctantly got to his feet. Alongside his interrogators, he cut a rather pathetic figure. About five feet eight inches tall, he had a lean, almost emaciated look. His general appearance was typical of a habitual drug abuser. His lank, dark brown hair stuck to his skin, saturated at the ends by the sweat now rolling freely down his face and neck. His thin arms, with no trace of muscle definition, hung limply by his sides. His grubby tee-shirt and low-slung tracksuit bottoms added to his generally unkempt appearance.

Spread out on the duvet in front of them, McIntyre and Lewis could see the unmistakeable paraphernalia of drug use. Two plain glass tubes, each about ten centimetres long, had what looked like steel wool wedged in at one end. The glass on the inside of one of the tubes had a smokier appearance than the other, which appeared clear. There was no mistaking what these objects were – crack pipes and one already appeared to have been used.

Also, on the duvet, next to the pipes, were four or five small, plastic resealable poly-grip bags. In each bag there appeared to be three or four small crystalline rocks, off-white in colour. Whilst speaking to Andrews earlier, McIntyre had also noticed several small squares of aluminium foil on the floor around the bed, which appeared to have scorch marks on them.

'Oh dear, right now things aren't looking too god for you, are they?' said McIntyre, feigning sympathy.

Andrews now looked completely disorientated by the sudden turn of events and McIntyre instinctively felt that a touch of the good cop at this stage would shortcut any lack of co-operation from the cowed young man. McIntyre picked up one of the bags off the duvet.

'Crack?' he asked. Andrews nodded in agreement.

'Apart from these in front of us, do you have any more on you, or anywhere else in the cabin?'

'No, that's it, that's all there is.'

'It's a very serious matter bringing illegal drugs on board a cruise ship, I hope you realise that. My colleague and I are now going to search you and your cabin for anything else which you shouldn't have. We would very much appreciate your co-operation with this, because if there is anything else here, we're going to find it.'

Andrews remained silent. He had been given his chance to reveal all.

'Right, first of all we need to see if you have anything on your person?'

Without further prompting, Andrews pulled off his tee-shirt, revealing his scrawny frame and raised his arms above his head.

He had done this before, it seemed. He flung the tee-shirt onto the bed and pulled the pockets outwards from his tracksuit bottoms, revealing them to be empty. He then stood with his arms outstretched by his sides.

'Good, now run your thumbs round the inside of your waistband; front, side and rear, like this,' said McIntyre, demonstrating the movement required on himself.

To McIntyre's surprise Andrews dropped his trousers completely to his ankles. He also dropped his boxer shorts and bent over in front of both men, whilst touching his toes. As he stood up, all but naked, he turned around, cupped his testicles in his right hand and raised them upwards.

His compliance came as a relief to McIntyre, who knew he had limited rights when it came to conducting a full body search. Andrews had made it easy for them.

'What I want you to do now is to take a seat over there by the desk, whilst we go through your belongings. I want you to watch very carefully what we're doing.'

During his police career, McIntyre had conducted thousands of searches like this and knew that occasionally, if incriminating items were found and the suspect wasn't present, allegations of planting evidence would be made.

Andrews was travelling light. The small wardrobe was practically empty and took little time to go through. Nothing of interest was found. McIntyre then reached under the bed and pulled out the rucksack he had seen earlier, before laying it on the bed.

'Are we likely to find anything in here, Lee?' he asked.

'Don't think so,' Andrews replied, rather unconvincingly.

Most of Andrews' clothing was still in the rucksack and

consisted mainly of tee-shirts, underwear and a couple of pairs of baggy jeans. Searching through one of the side pockets of the rucksack, McIntyre came upon a small plastic poly-bag, slightly bigger than the ones containing the rocks. This bag was full of white powder.

'Is this what I think it is?' asked McIntyre.

'Yeah, it's coke,' Andrews replied, the realisation of his plight rapidly dawning on him.

'Before I started searching your rucksack, I asked you if there was anything in it. By that I meant anything there shouldn't be, like cocaine for starters. Why didn't you tell me it was here? What else am I likely to find?'

'I just forgot it was there, I wasn't trying to hide anything,' Andrews replied lamely.

A thorough search of the rest of the main cabin yielded nothing further of interest.

'We're going to have a look in the bathroom now,' continued McIntyre. 'Again, I'm asking you, are we going to find any more drugs in there?'

'Looks like it's all come on top,' sighed Andrews. 'I'll come clean with you. I'm a recovering heroin addict, my methadone script is in my toilet bag. You'll also find some diazepam there as well. I've got a script for them too. I've managed to stay off the smack for quite a while now but unfortunately I've started on the coke and the crack which is just as bad.'

Searching the cramped bathroom didn't take long. McIntyre stood at the entrance with Andrews, whilst Lewis conducted the search. Just as Andrews had admitted, Lewis found two small bottles in his toilet bag. The labels on both bottles were marked *Methadose oral concentrate 10mg* and bore Andrews' name, as well as the dispensing chemist's address, which was located in Andrews' home town. There appeared little doubt that this was a genuine prescription.

Also in the toilet bag, Lewis found another clear plastic poly-bag. Inside the bag was a large number of small, round white tablets, each with a score through the middle on one side. On the opposite side of each tablet was the figure ten and some lettering. The tablets were loose. Lewis passed the items to McIntyre.

'I take it this is the methadone?' said McIntyre, indicating the bottles, 'What are the tablets in the bag?'

'That's the diazepam I told you about.'

'How come they're all loose like that? If they were prescribed to you, I would expect to see them in blister packs. There's nothing there to prove they've been prescribed to you like the methadone.'

'It's easier to carry them like that. I popped them all out and just put them in the bag. I've just realised I left the boxes at home, but they were definitely on my script.'

From McIntyre's knowledge of controlled drugs, gleaned through many years' experience, he knew that methadone was an opioid, whilst diazepam belonged to the benzodiazepine group of drugs.

He was also aware that very often with drug addicts, the use of both types of drug simultaneously, adversely affected the efficacy of either, or both. He harboured serious doubts therefore that the tablets which Andrews claimed to be diazepam, had been legally prescribed to him.

Whilst searching Andrews' accommodation, both men had noticed smears of blood on his pillow and the top of the duvet cover. Both towels in the bathroom also had areas of bloodstaining.

'Where's all this this blood come from?' McIntyre asked the now visibly shaking young man.

'It's from the cut on my nose. Every time I wash or have a shower, it starts to bleed again.'

'Ok Lee. You don't need me to tell you that you're now in a very serious spot of bother. First of all, you are in possession of a considerable quantity of what you yourself have admitted are controlled drugs. That's very serious in itself, but the other issue that greatly concerns us, is that you appear to be one of the last people to have seen Anne on board the ship before she disappeared. There's bloodstaining throughout the cabin which you may have given a reasonable explanation for, but there's an awful lot for us to be concerned about with you. Do you understand that?'

'Yeah, I see where you're coming from. It doesn't look good. You've got me bang to rights for the drugs, apart from the methadone and the benzos, but I swear to God I haven't a clue what's happened to her. Like I said, I've only seen her twice since we've been on the ship.'

'We're going to have to speak to the captain about your situation.' McIntyre went on. 'In the meantime, I'm going to have to ask you to come down to the security office with us, whilst we decide what's going to happen to you.'

Whilst Lewis remained in the cabin, McIntyre escorted Andrews down to the security office. He placed him in the small interview room where they had previously spoken to Leonard, before delegating a member of his security staff to remain with him at all times, even if he requested to use the toilet.

He then returned to the cabin where he assisted Lewis in bagging and sealing the drugs which they had already found. After a short discussion, both men agreed the cabin would have to be preserved as a possible crime scene. They intended to have it photographed and swabbed at the earliest opportunity, particularly the areas with bloodstaining. As they left the room, McIntyre affixed another *Do Not Enter* sticker to the door.

They now had two potential crime scenes.

12

By now, McIntyre and Lewis were extremely tired, but a progress meeting was hastily arranged to take place in the incident room back on Deck 14. McIntyre had retained the use of this room, as it was nearer for Captain Alex and the staff captain, Konstantinos, to get to, without taking them too far from the bridge. As McIntyre and Lewis waited, Konstantinos was the first to arrive, shortly followed by Captain Alex and Samaras, the safety officer.

'How's the search going, gentlemen? Anything positive to report?' asked Captain Alex in his usual direct manner.

Lewis remained silent as McIntyre replied. He was acutely aware, especially in the captain's presence, that as a non-crew member his involvement was unusual to say the least and he judged it best to remain silent, unless his opinion was actively sought.

'Following on from our discovery yesterday that there are four passengers travelling in Anne's group, Mr Lewis and I have had a very busy and productive day. We've interviewed the husband for the second time, but he has nothing further to add to what he told us last night. We've also traced and spoken to the other two passengers listed in the party, two guys by the names of Craig Leonard and Lee Andrews. All three staterooms have been searched and I can state categorically she's not in any of them.'

'Having spoken to the three of them, do you have any better idea of what might have happened to Mrs Ebsworth?' Captain Alex continued. 'Today's Thursday and we'll be reaching New York by early Monday morning. We don't have much time left to discover where she might have disappeared to.'

'We're going to need to speak to all three again, because I feel sure the key to her disappearance lies with one of them, although there's still the possibility she could have jumped or fallen overboard. Her husband told us she was under a lot of stress at work. He also seemed to be completely unaware his wife had booked and paid for the other two passengers. When we showed him the invoice, he said he didn't know either of them and appeared genuinely shocked.

I got the impression they weren't very close as a couple, but he does seem extremely upset she's gone missing. Although he's in a wheelchair, he still looks pretty fit, but if he's harmed her in any way, he would have had to have done it in the stateroom, but there's no evidence of a struggle.

Let's assume however, if he did harm her and she was unable to leave the stateroom, the only way he could have disposed of her body would have been by pushing her over the balcony.

He certainly appears to have the upper body strength to have done that and the position of the balcony on the midship bulge would make it relatively easy for the body to fall straight down into the sea, without striking any of the other decks, but there are some lifeboats below the balcony which could have arrested her fall.

What I'm saying in relation to him therefore, is that he can't be ruled out as a suspect at this stage.'

'And the other two?' Captain Alex leant forward, listening intently.

'Craig Leonard is interesting. He was a bit reticent to begin with, but he eventually confirmed to us that the reason he's here is because he and Anne are lovers. I need to do a bit more digging into his background because there's just something about him that makes me feel uneasy.

Mike here agrees with me. Leonard's an ex-soldier and is now working in a gym, which is apparently where they met, about a year ago. He reckons Dean Ebsworth is unaware his wife was having an affair with him and that certainly seems to tie in with Dean's reaction when we showed him the invoice.

According to Leonard, they last met the night Anne went missing, but he claims he hasn't seen her since. Of course, we have definite CCTV footage of them together around the time she went missing and in fact he is the very last person to be seen in her company.

A definite suspect I'd say.'

'Ok and the other guy, what did you say his name was?'

'Lee Andrews. We have a major problem with him. He told us he used to work at the same company as Anne. According to him, that's how he got to know her. However, there's a lot more to it than that I'm sure. He's admitted himself he's a recovering heroin addict and he's on a methadone programme.

We found his methadone prescription, but we also found cocaine powder, some crack cocaine and what we believe to be diazepam tablets. Just looking at him, I'd say he has a very serious drug habit and in fact I'm a little bit disappointed we didn't flag him up when he came on board at Southampton. If we had done, we may have discovered the drugs he was carrying and refused him boarding. I suspect the reason we missed him was because he may have boarded when it was very busy.

The other significant thing about him is that he has some nasty facial injuries, which he said were caused by falling down stairs. He might be telling the truth on that, but I have my doubts. There's also quite a lot of blood staining in his cabin, which may be related to his injuries. He says he's only seen Anne twice whilst on board, the last time being late Monday afternoon. Again, it appears Dean Ebsworth hasn't a clue who Andrews is.'

'Where is he now? Captain Alex enquired.

'He's down in the security office, with one of my officers keeping an eye on him. We need to decide what we're going to do with him. I think we've found all the drugs he had with him, but if we confine him to his cabin, he's going to go cold turkey and he'll just become a nuisance. He definitely won't stay put.'

'What are you suggesting we do with him?'

'Well sir, at the end of the day it's your decision as captain, but he's obviously breached his conditions of boarding by being in possession of controlled drugs and I think there's a reasonable inference to be drawn that he may have something to do with Anne's disappearance. I think there's a strong case to be made for keeping him in the brig.'

Captain Alex sat back in his chair and exhaled loudly through clenched teeth, followed by a long sigh. McIntyre had given him a difficult decision to make.

Like most large cruise ships, Enterprise Endeavour had a

couple of rooms in the security section which were fitted out as cells. Since all rooms on board ship were made of metal, the walls and ceilings of these cells were fitted with padding and contained no furniture other than a sleeping platform, attached to one wall. The cells also contained a small bathroom cubicle, with only a sink and toilet. Most passengers were completely unaware of the existence of these facilities.

The criteria for using them was strict. A passenger, or not infrequently, a crew member, would only be confined there for a serious infraction of ship board rules, such as fighting, extreme drunkenness, serious assault, drug dealing etc. If the offender could be confined to their cabin, then that was the preferred option and incarceration in the brig was used very much as a last resort.

Normally anyone finding themselves there could expect to be handed over to the relevant law enforcement agencies at the next port of call, or escorted off the ship, with no prospect of return. As a general rule in the cruise line industry, but particularly on American flagged ships, these cells were known by the old naval term, *the brig*.

Captain Alex sat with his elbows on the table in front of him, his forehead resting against his hands, his knuckles showing white above his tightly interlocked fingers. He appeared lost in thought, as though elsewhere.

McIntyre couldn't be sure, but he had heard persistent rumours the captain had a drug-addicted son back in Greece. What he did know for certain, from previous experience of working with him, was that the captain was vehemently anti-drugs, particularly in relation to misuse on board a ship under his command. After a lengthy pause, he leaned back in his chair.

'Do you think he brought the drugs on board with him, or is there any suggestion he could have acquired them after boarding the ship?'

'Obviously we need to speak to him again and I'll try to clarify that point, but I'm pretty sure he came prepared and the drugs were already in his possession when he boarded.'

'In that case, I don't have a problem with authorising his detention in the brig until we reach landfall. I'm particularly concerned about his possession of the crack cocaine which I understand to be a particularly addictive drug. I've heard t it makes the users very unpredictable and potentially dangerous. We can't have him loose on the ship in these circumstances.'

'Thank you for that, captain. I'll make the necessary arrangements as soon as I leave here.'

McIntyre had anticipated this response and had noted the sadness in the captain's expression when he was considering his decision. Perhaps the rumours about his son were true after all.

'So, what's the plan of action going forward?' Captain Alex enquired.

'I don't think there's much more we can do tonight,' replied McIntyre. 'I know the ship's been thoroughly searched already, but I'd like a second search to be made in case anything's been overlooked. Perhaps that can be arranged for tomorrow. Mike and I will also interview Dean Ebsworth, Leonard and Andrews again tomorrow and hopefully put a bit more pressure on them.

I want to go through the Ebsworth stateroom again to try to build a better picture of Anne, because it's beginning to appear there's more to her background than we currently know. Mike and I also have a diary and some paperwork from the stateroom which we'll have a look through tonight before we finish.'

'Well, you appear to have it all under control,' said Captain Alex, rising to his feet. 'I'll see you all at morning prayers. Good evening, gentlemen and thank you for your efforts.'

Konstantinos and Samaras waited until the captain had left before making tracks to follow.

'Are you sure there's nothing we can do to help?' said Konstantinos as he reached the door.

From his obvious haste to leave, it was evident he was hoping for a negative response. McIntyre duly obliged.

'Not at the moment, but we'll probably need some help co-ordinating a second search of the ship tomorrow. We'll catch up then.'

It was now almost midnight and both McIntyre and Lewis had been busy since early morning. For McIntyre this was nothing unusual. The life of a crew member normally involved at least twelve-hour shifts, in his case often much longer, seven days a week. Lewis's itinerary as a guest speaker was far less demanding however and of the two, he felt the least drained and the adrenalin rush of the investigation had meant the day had passed very quickly for him.

'How about a swift one down in the crew bar whilst we decide what we're going to do next?' suggested McIntyre.

'Thought you'd never ask - although being a Scotsman, I suppose you'll have the usual short arms and deep pockets,' laughed Lewis.

The crew bar was located at the stern of the vessel on deck zero. Considering this was the social hub of the ship, with a crew of around fifteen-hundred, it was surprisingly compact.

The room spanned the entire width of the ship, but was fairly narrow. The actual bar area itself was located along the port side wall and featured lots of highly polished mahogany. Dotted around the room, fairly close together, was a collection of tables with assorted chairs and low stools. A waist-high shelf ran the entire length of the starboard wall, with a line of bar stools positioned along it.

The back of the room led out onto an open deck area, about four metres deep, directly overlooking the ship's stern. This area was shielded from view from above by a fixed canopy which stopped about a metre short of the stern rail. It was perhaps just as well this space was not overlooked from the passenger accommodation, as it was the scene of many raucous nights, with crew members winding down after an arduous day's work.

As an officer, McIntyre was entitled to use any of the ship's bars in the passenger areas, but he rarely did. Oddly enough, most of his fellow officers, apart from the most senior, did likewise. Apart from the fact that the drinks in the crew bar were far cheaper, there were other factors to be considered.

McIntyre had always had an eye for the ladies and the crew bar afforded endless opportunities. Fraternisation with passengers by crew members was forbidden on practically all cruise ships and this rule was strictly enforced. No such restrictions were placed on relationships between crew members however, provided they took place beyond the public areas.

Also, as chief security officer, McIntyre used his trips to the crew bar as an opportunity to keep an informal eye on the antics of his crew mates, although he was by no means a killjoy.

As they entered the crew bar, Lewis was immediately struck by how crowded it was, despite the fact it had by now gone midnight. Large groups were gathered around the tables placed throughout the room.

Some of the groups seemed to consist of the same nationality. At a glance he could see groups of what he thought looked like Albanians, Filipinos and Indian or Pakistani nationals. The most striking feature of the clientele however appeared to be their sheer diversity.

From previous conversations with McIntyre, he already knew this crew consisted of over sixty different nationalities. Apart from the larger groups, the rest of the crew appeared to be mixing freely and revelling in each other's company. He found it difficult to imagine such a relaxed scenario being enacted on shore.

McIntyre moved ahead and headed straight for the open area overlooking the stern. As he threaded his way through the crowded bar, Lewis noticed the deferential nods in McIntyre's direction from several of the drinkers. He also seemed to attract the attention of more than one of the females in the room. This came as no surprise to Lewis, who was all too aware of his colleague's colourful history.

Although now well into his fifties, McIntyre still exuded an impressive presence. Standing just over six feet tall, he had retained the broad shouldered, rugged build, forged by his island heritage. His once black hair was now speckled with grey and fashionably cut in a neat, crew-cut style. His strong features were accentuated by a closely trimmed beard and moustache. He was obviously very well-known and respected on board.

Once outside, McIntyre headed for a small table in a corner by the port rail, underneath the overhang. A couple of crew members already sitting there got up and moved away as he approached, with no words being spoken. Lewis guessed this was McIntyre's regular spot. He gestured for Lewis to sit down.

'Right Mike, I'll get them in. Short pockets indeed. What's your poison?'

'Well since we're in the crew bar, it would probably be appropriate to have a tot of rum don't you think?'

'Indeed, me hearty, 'chuckled McIntyre, effecting his best pirate's imitation.

After a few minutes, McIntyre returned with a couple of large glasses of dark rum and four small bottles of beer.

'I think we deserve these after the day we've had. There's still a lot to be done, so let's enjoy a drink and see what tomorrow brings.'

For a short while, neither man spoke. Lewis guessed that by now they were in mid-Atlantic and this low down on the ship he could feel the steady pulse of the twin propellers, which he estimated were almost directly beneath them. He could see the wake streaming out behind them, a maelstrom of white foam, speckled with colour from the reflection of the ship's lights, in sharp contrast to the blackness of the ocean. Lewis's thoughts took him back to his childhood in Devon when he used to sit outside on dark nights such as this.

'You look like you're away with the fairies Mike. You all right?'

'Yeah, just enjoying the moment. It's so fresh and peaceful out here. We're surrounded by people and yet it feels as if we're all alone.'

'I know what you mean. I love it here, especially after a hard day. It's a great place to unwind.'

As they enjoyed their drinks, both men quietly carried on

people watching. As ex-police officers, this was a habit they found hard to kick. McIntyre tried to explain the social politics being played out before them.

Why did the Albanians always seem to stick together? He didn't have an answer, but guessed it was just something in their national psyche, or perhaps it was difficulty in conversing in English, the universal language on board.

The Filipinos, he knew, formed a sort of ship-board mafia, particularly the seamen. They exerted a lot of influence in the crew areas and were naturally suspicious of the security department, although not in an overtly hostile way.

During his relatively short time in ships' security, McIntyre had learned a lot about what made the many different nationalities on board tick. Lewis listened in fascination. Like most cruise passengers, he was aware of the crew's diversity, but he had never given it much thought before. Down here, it was all laid out before him, a living microcosm of humanity.

'I know you've got your lecture to deliver in the morning, Mike, so whilst you're doing that, I'll attend morning prayers and hopefully get another search of the ship set up and maybe have another look through the Ebsworth's stateroom. In the meantime, I'd be grateful if you could have a look through Anne's diary for me. It's one of those three-year ones I took from their stateroom the other night. There's some other paperwork as well, but I'll attend to that.'

They slowly finished their drinks, taking time to enjoy the ambience that surrounded them, before finally returning to their cabins. It was the end of a long day but there was still much work to be done.

13

As he lay on his bed, McIntyre picked up the folder of correspondence he had taken from the Ebsworth's stateroom. By now he was very tired but knew time was of the essence in the search for Anne. Perhaps there was something in the folder that would reveal more. She had been almost the sole focus of his attention for the past couple of days, but at that moment he realised he knew very little about her.

To all outward appearances, she seemed fairly unremarkable. He had seen her security photographs and the CCTV stills of the night she went missing. Nothing about her appeared anything other than normal. But, as he had heard from her husband, she was under a lot of stress.

Was this due to something happening at work? The existence of a lover, of whom her husband was almost certainly unaware? And what exactly was her relationship with Lee Andrews? Then there was the designer wardrobe, which coupled with her paying for all four in the party to travel, suggested money was not in short supply. Perhaps most intriguingly of all though, was the fact that, apart from Anne, they all seemed to be unaware of each other's existence.

There were a lot of questions he needed to find the answers to.

Most of the correspondence appeared to relate to the Ebsworth's domestic finances, virtually all of which appeared to be in her name. Why did she even have them with her?

Bank statements going back three months showed mortgage payments of over one thousand pounds per month, together with numerous other standing order and direct debit payments. In the credit column, the sum of approximately two thousand five hundred pounds per month was regularly paid in by Ace Valves, which McIntyre took to be her salary.

Despite this, her outgoings would have far exceeded her income were it not for a monthly deposit of five thousand pounds, which appeared to be transferred in from another account. This payment only just kept the current account in credit every month. Clearly, Anne had another substantial source of income, which was not detailed in these statements.

McIntyre knew he would probably be speaking to Dean again later on in the day and he made a mental note to ask him what he knew of his wife's finances. Since there was no evidence to show the couple held a joint bank account, it was possible he may know very little.

Finding little else of interest, McIntyre finally gave way to sleep. He knew he would be up and about again in a little over four hours.

At just after six o'clock on the Friday morning, McIntyre was back in the security control room. Whilst the Ebsworth enquiry had occupied the bulk of his time since he had first been summoned to the meeting with the captain on the Wednesday morning, he still had his normal duties to attend to, which in themselves ensured he was always kept busy.

The one redeeming feature of this particular cruise however, was the number of consecutive sea days whilst crossing the Atlantic. Sea days brought their own set of challenges for the security department, since all passengers and crew were on board ship for the entire day. Passengers tended to drink more, which in turn led to added potential for disorder and accidents.

Likewise, incidents involving crew members were more likely to occur when they were under pressure. On the positive side however, was the fact that his department didn't have to deal with the added stress of passengers and crew coming and going from the ship, as they would if the vessel was in port.

For the next couple of hours McIntyre busied himself with the various administrative tasks associated with running his department, knowing the rest of the day would once again be mainly concerned with the search for Anne.

At around half past eight, he made his way to the crew mess for breakfast. He could have used the officers' mess, but generally utilised the crew mess because he preferred to eat with his staff. Also, a big part of the security department's role was to be the captain's eyes and ears throughout the ship and McIntyre considered the best way to carry out this role was to be visible but discreet at all times.

The food in the crew mess was surprisingly good, even though it did feature a lot of recycled items from the passenger menus to make curries, stews and similar dishes which could be easily reheated. Whatever was on the menu however, was always accompanied by mountains of boiled rice, which was particularly favoured by the Asian and Filipino crew members. McIntyre never ceased to marvel at the sheer quantity of rice they consumed, no matter what the meal consisted of, or what time of day it was eaten.

By nine o'clock, McIntyre was seated around the low table in the captain's stateroom along with his fellow attendees, awaiting the start of morning prayers. On the stroke of nine, Captain Alex joined them.

During his short presentation to the group, McIntyre mentioned he had previously discussed with the captain the possibility of conducting a second search of the ship for the missing passenger. Very little else of note appeared to have taken place and the captain prepared to bring the meeting to a close after barely fifteen minutes.

'I have no doubt that a thorough search of the ship was carried out on Wednesday morning,' the captain said, as he glanced around the table, 'but our passenger is still missing and we are no nearer to finding out what's happened to her. I agree with Mr McIntyre that a second search should be carried out as soon as possible. I'll leave it to each head of department to make the necessary arrangements in liaison with the security department. You can understand I'm very keen to get to the bottom of this,' the captain concluded, before leaving the room.

Before everyone else moved on, McIntyre conducted a very quick briefing, reminding those present of the description of the missing passenger and requesting they showed her photograph to as many of the crew as possible.

He decided against updating them with details of Leonard and Andrews, since they couldn't yet be definitively linked to Anne's disappearance and he knew how easily wild rumours could circulate around the ship. He was also aware of course, that by now, news of Anne being missing would be common knowledge amongst the crew and he was keen for that to continue, since the more pairs of eyes that were looking for her, the better.

Stepping from the lift back down on deck zero, McIntyre walked along a short passageway, before coming to a wide T-junction. Turning either right or left would take him onto the longest single gangway on the entire ship. This gangway was approximately three metres wide and ran from bow to stern, a length of just over three hundred metres.

At various points along its length were huge steel doors, effectively dividing the ship into watertight compartments when closed. The position of these doors was marked by highly visible yellow and black-chevroned ramps on the floor, on the entry and egress sides of the doors. On the Enterprise Endeavour, as on most US operated ships, this gangway was commonly referred to as the *I-95*.

When he had first heard the expression, McIntyre was unaware of what it meant, until it was pointed out to him it could signify two things.

Mainly, it was a nod to *Interstate 95*, one of the most famous roads in the United States. Covering a distance of almost two thousand miles, the I-95 runs north to south along the eastern seaboard of America, roughly parallel to the Atlantic Ocean. It links with many major cities along its route, including Boston, New York, Philadelphia, Washington D.C., Jacksonville and Miami.

Alternatively, *Form I-95* is a document issued by US Customs & Border Protection, as a Crewman's Landing Permit. Form I-95 is therefore a very well-known document by crew members on cruise ships sailing in and out of the United States.

As McIntyre glanced in both directions along the length of

the gangway, he was struck, as always, by how busy it was. He had entered the I-95 midships and had only a few paces to walk until he came to the loading bay, which occupied a huge space, roughly the size of a tennis court, on either side of the gangway. This was the area where all the ship's supplies were loaded and on port days, as he knew from experience, it was absolute mayhem.

Being a sea day however, activity was a little less frantic, as most of the supplies had been moved to their respective store rooms. Nevertheless, several fork lift trucks were busy around this area, moving pallets to the service lifts and between stores. The I-95 in this particular area was quite a dangerous place to be if crew members didn't have their wits about them, as the fork lift drivers, although highly skilled, raced around at top speed.

As he walked through the loading bay, McIntyre caught sight of the loadmaster, Ahmad, an Indonesian. He was easily recognisable, even from a distance, as he was almost as wide as he was tall. Since he was no more than five foot six inches in height, this gave Ahmad a distinctly rotund appearance. His girth was further accentuated by his white boiler suit and the padded over jacket he was wearing. This was topped off by a dark woolly hat and McIntyre noticed he was also wearing heavy duty, industrial gloves. From the way he was dressed, it appeared the loadmaster may have been working in or near one of the many cold stores.

As McIntyre approached him, Ahmad greeted him with his customary beaming smile and a hearty high-five. Ahmad was one of the crew's larger-than-life characters and despite the full-on nature of his job, McIntyre never saw him without a smile on his face.

'How's it going my friend?' said Ahmad, 'You've caught up with me at last. How did you know it was me?'

He grinned mischievously at his joking inference he had committed some imaginary offence.

'Always a pleasure, Ahmad. Of course, you're not in any trouble, unless there's something I don't know about, in which case I'll be back. You know I always get my man,' McIntyre countered, carrying on the joke.

'So, what brings the security chief to my little patch of heaven?'

'You know we have a missing passenger and a couple of days ago we requested a search of the whole ship to try to find her. Were you involved in that at all?'

'Yes, my boss asked me to search all our stores which we did, but we found nothing.'

'Ok, well you'll be getting another request very shortly to do it all again, because she still hasn't been found. I'd very much appreciate your help with this.'

'It'll take a while, but since it's a sea day, we're not too stretched. I'll get something organised right away, boss.'

McIntyre knew the loadmaster decanted the ship's supplies into over forty different stores, so the search of his area would take some time and manpower. The main reason for the multiplicity of store rooms was that each room was dedicated to one product only, to avoid cross contamination, particularly of food items.

He also knew a large number of the store rooms were refrigerated to various different temperatures, making them ideal places to temporarily conceal and preserve a body, pending eventual disposal.

The fish store for example, was kept at a constant temperature of minus twenty-three degrees Celsius, whilst the cheese store was a more tolerable minus eight degrees. Crew members entering these stores had to take special precautions and had to wear appropriate clothing, which protected against the extreme cold. Getting trapped in one of these store rooms could result in death within a very short period of time.

Glancing at his watch, McIntyre noticed it was not yet ten o'clock and he knew it would be at least another hour before Mike Lewis had finished his lecture in the ship's theatre. He decided to use the time productively to check any other areas below the passenger decks where someone could possibly be hidden. By now, although he had no evidence to back it up, he was convinced he was looking for a body.

He could think of no reason why areas of the ship open to crew only would be chosen as a hiding place, other than the multiplicity of spaces and store rooms, where there would be relatively few people around at certain times.

His next stop was with the Environmental Officer, Stavros Pavlides. The EO was, like most of the ship's officers, a Greek national. He had been at morning prayers a few minutes earlier and had just returned to his office when McIntyre entered.

The role of the environmental officer was a vitally important one on the ship. His main areas of responsibility were the supply of fresh drinking water and the disposal of all the waste produced on board. Drinking water was obtained by ingesting seawater via pumps in the ship's hull, then passing it through a desalinisation plant.

The disposal of waste was a more complicated process. Waste consisted of sewage and other types of waste such as glass, cans, plastic, metal, cardboard and food.

The sewage consisted of 'grey water' from galleys, bathrooms and the laundry and 'black water' from the lavatories. This was mixed together in measured proportions, before being passed through a macerator, which subjected the waste to an exhaustive biological process. Solids left behind from this process were stored on board in tanks until they could be off-loaded in port.

Providing the ship was at least twelve miles offshore and travelling at a speed of more than six knots, the rest of the waste was discharged at sea. In the case of non-sewage waste, this was generally baled and eventually also off-loaded in port. Most waste food could also be macerated and disposed of at sea in a similar way to sewage.

McIntyre was particularly interested in the area where the bales and storage tanks were kept and in particular the garbage cold store, which was kept at a temperature of minus thirty-one degrees Celsius, since he felt this would be an ideal spot to conceal a body. Additionally, an unpleasant odour pervaded the general area, which would undoubtedly mask the smell of any decomposition which might take place.

Pavlides gave McIntyre his assurance that a further search was about to be carried out as requested, particularly since a large number of bales had been added to the storage area since the last search a couple of days previously.

Moving two decks further down, to the very bowels of the ship, McIntyre came to the laundry. The laundry was hot and stuffy and due to the heavy-duty machinery, which operated continuously throughout the day, particularly noisy. The laundry catered for the needs of all passengers and crew, although many of the crew members did their own.

On any given day, up to one hundred tons of laundry would be processed, sea days being the busiest. Although he felt it unlikely a body could remain here for long, mainly due to the heat, McIntyre was aware that due to the sheer volume of material which passed through the area, it was nevertheless possible. He also knew the laundry arrived in large, wheeled trolleys, which would make it reasonably easy to conceal and transport a body from any area of the ship.

He made a point of seeking out Anil, who was in charge of the laundry, to appraise him of the need for a second search. Besides, he had a great deal of respect for the crew who worked in this area. They had perhaps one of the hardest jobs on the ship and very rarely saw the light of day.

Satisfied that a second search of the ship would be underway soon, McIntyre returned to the security control room to await the end of Mike Lewis's lecture. As he got there, he heard loud banging coming from the brig, interspersed with muffled shouting.

He had almost forgotten that Lee Andrews was still confined there and would continue to be, until the ship reached New York. Grabbing a set of keys from the wall safe, he went towards the brig and opened the door to Andrews' cell. As he entered, he noticed the young man's forehead was a vivid red colour, which he assumed had been caused by him continuously banging his head against the door, which was the only area of the cell which wasn't padded. Andrews was also shaking and sweating profusely.

Cold turkey had well and truly set in.

'Get me fucking out of here, I ain't done nothing wrong. Why am I being treated like a fucking criminal?' he whimpered, before sitting back down on his bunk where he began to rock back and forth, his knees drawn tightly under his chin and his arms wrapped round his shins.

'You know you're going to have to stay here for at least a couple more days, Lee,' said McIntyre soothingly. 'I'll get the nurse to come up and give you something to calm you down. We'll also be coming back to speak to you again a bit later on.'

He had seen many drug addicts in custody during the course of his career and wasn't unsympathetic to his plight, but he knew Andrews would be a constant nuisance to his staff until they made landfall.

14

Making his way back up to Deck 5, McIntyre rendez-voused with Lewis in their favourite coffee bar, as Lewis had just finished his lecture. The prospect of another busy day lay ahead and coffee was an imperative.

'After I left you last night, I had a look through some of the correspondence I initially took from the Ebsworth stateroom,' McIntyre began. 'She appears to control their finances and there's a few things that just don't add up. It also looks like she's spending far more than she's earning, but there's five thousand a month going into her account from somewhere else that I haven't been able to figure out yet.'

'I may be able to help you out there,' Lewis replied.' I started to look through the diary you gave me to examine. I began with the most recent year first and that's about as far as I've got. I need to spend a bit more time on it, but a couple of things leapt out at me.

It appears she may have been embezzling money from her company, because various entries relate to figures at the back of the diary, which refer to the Ace account and some of the cryptic entries suggest she feels guilty about what she's been doing. If I've interpreted the figures correctly and what they appear to represent, the total amount of her fraud may run into something in the region of about two hundred thousand pounds.

If that isn't surprising enough, there's more. There are frequent references to meeting someone referred to only as LA, and abbreviated weights and single letters, which I now believe to be different types and quantities of drugs. If I was a betting man, I'd say she has been buying drugs, whether for herself or someone else.

It may just be a coincidence, but I think LA might be our druggy friend, Lee Andrews. The other thing that was mentioned quite regularly in her diary is the fact she appears to have been subjected to a fair amount of domestic abuse by Dean, mental and physical, over a lengthy period of time.'

As both men drank their coffee, they were in total agreement on one thing. Anne Ebsworth appeared to have been leading a very complicated life. Not only did she have a disabled husband who appeared to abuse her, a secret lover and a drug-using acquaintance whom she was in all probability buying drugs from, but it now also appeared she may also have been stealing large amounts of money from her employer.

Whilst her initial disappearance may have been unexplained, there were now several very good reasons to believe that finding her alive was becoming an increasingly remote possibility.

'Now that we know a lot more about her than we did even yesterday,' McIntyre continued, 'let's have a look at the various scenarios that could have taken place. Let's start with the assumption she could have committed suicide. What are your thoughts on that, Mike?'

'There's certainly enough reasons for her to have contemplated taking her own life. We know she's been under a lot of stress, not just from what Dean's told us, but from what we've both learned over the past twenty-four hours. There are several reasons which would suggest that hasn't happened however.

Firstly, the most obvious way to do it would be by jumping overboard, but we've come up with absolutely no evidence to suggest she's done that. If she didn't jump overboard, how else could she have done it? Drug overdose? Perhaps, but where would she have taken them and why hasn't she been found? Also, I didn't find anything in her diary to suggest she was suicidal. Remorseful perhaps, but not suicidal.

However, you know the golden rule. Never rule anything out until you are absolutely certain.'

'I'm more or less in agreement with you on that assessment,' McIntyre pondered, 'but there are certainly more than enough reasons for her to have taken her own life. I'm just praying we haven't missed anything on CCTV. Ruling out suicide for the moment however, let's move on to who could have a motive for harming her. Dean would seem to be a good starting point?'

'For sure. You and I both know from the murder enquiries we've been involved in the majority of these offences are committed by someone very close to the victim, very often either the partner or another family member.

From the evidence we have so far, he appears to have a history of violence towards her. If he's aware she has a lover, it would give him a very clear motive for causing her harm. However, from the brief conversations we've had with him, he didn't give me the impression that he knows about either Leonard or Andrews.

Also, what if anything does he know about her apparently stealing from work? Could that be something which troubled him? Even allowing for his lack of mobility, he still appears capable of having caused her harm, but I just can't see how he would have had the opportunity to do so and dispose of her body on board this ship. The only way he could possibly have done it would have been by tipping her over their balcony.

We really need to have another chat with Dean as soon as possible and complete the search of their stateroom to see if there's anything we may have missed. As far as I'm concerned, the jury's still out on Dean.'

'Pretty much with you on that as well, Mike. Shall we move on to Craig Leonard?' McIntyre said, as he beckoned the waiter over to bring another round of coffees.

'Tricky one, this,' continued Lewis, leaning forward slightly with both elbows on the table, his interlocked hands pressed tightly against his forehead.

'I didn't particularly warm to him when we spoke to him yesterday. Seemed a bit sure of himself and a bit resentful of authority, but that could be down to his previous dealings with the police and maybe even his military background. But not liking someone doesn't make him a suspect. There has to be something else. There's no question they've been lovers, but why would he want to harm her? A lovers' tiff perhaps? Jealousy?

The main thing that puts him in the frame is he's the last person to have been seen with her immediately prior to her disappearance and the fact he doesn't seem to be overly concerned that she's missing. Definitely can't rule him out.'

'I can't figure him out either. Plays it with a bit of a poker face, but he was definitely nervous when we interviewed him, although he tried his best to hide it. I was also a bit suspicious at how tidy his stateroom was. It looked as though it had been thoroughly gone over, but his explanation of being in the military could be a simple explanation. I've known a few ex-military types who were almost obsessively tidy. It's bred into them. We definitely need to do a follow up interview with him.

Now we come to our little friend languishing in the brig, Lee Andrews. What's your take on him?'

'When we spoke to him yesterday, I was having great difficulty getting my head round his reason for being on board. Ex-colleague of Anne's, always fancied going on a cruise, so she very conveniently invites him along and says he can pay her back later. Just didn't ring true to me.

At the time I thought she must have known he's a junkie, as you only need to look at him to see that. Having now read part of her diary however, it's all beginning to make sense. I'm beginning to think he's definitely been supplying her with drugs, probably cocaine and maybe some of the diazepam tablets, if that's what they really are. I doubt if she'd be smoking crack. That and the methadone is probably for his own use.

I'm not sure what motive he would have to cause her harm however. After all, she appears to have been looking after him pretty well, apart from sticking him in that pokey cabin. You don't bite the hand that feeds you, do you?'

'Indeed. That diary has opened up a whole new can of worms though,' said McIntyre, as he sat back in his chair and drained his coffee. 'Obviously we'd never considered the fact Anne may have been taking drugs up to this point. Given the chaos in her life that appears to be emerging however, it's maybe not surprising. Unless you have any other ideas, I suggest we have another look round the Ebsworth stateroom, now that it's daylight, then I think we need to schedule another interview today with all three of them. Looks like it's going to be another long one, Mike. A life on the ocean waves and all that!'

Whilst Lewis returned to his stateroom to once more change out of his 'stage' clothes, McIntyre went back to the security office, primarily to check on the welfare of Lee Andrews.

As he entered the control room, one of the ship's doctors was just making her way from the direction of the brig. After a short conversation, McIntyre learned the doctor had taken the decision to continue prescribing methadone to Andrews, under controlled conditions, since she was satisfied the methadone already found in his possession had been legally prescribed.

McIntyre was pleased at this, as it would keep Andrews on some sort of even keel until they reached port. Having been told by the doctor that Andrews was now calm, he decided against opening his cell for the time being.

Several minutes later both men reconvened outside stateroom 1249, on Deck 10, the original Ebsworth stateroom. Since the pass key entry system had been disabled, McIntyre called one of the ship's electricians to help them gain entry to the cabin, which had not been entered since McIntyre's last visit. Once inside, the investigators immediately made their way to the balcony.

This time it was broad daylight. As they were now just past mid-Atlantic, a heavy swell was quite noticeable, particularly now they were out in the open. The horizon rose and fell perceptibly in the far distance and again the ocean seemed vast and empty.

As both men stood looking over the balcony rail, the

desolation around them seemed to add to the sense of mystery and intrigue surrounding Anne's disappearance.

A close examination of the balcony revealed no obvious signs that a struggle had taken place. The highly polished wooden rail was smooth and devoid of scratches and the glass panelling to the front and sides appeared unblemished, apart from the slight staining by the salt spray that was borne there by the constant wind.

The rail itself was just over four feet high. Whilst Lewis sat on one of the balcony chairs, to mimic the effect of being in a wheelchair, he attempted to hoist McIntyre over the side. McIntyre of course resisted, just as he imagined Anne would have done had she not already been incapacitated. To the surprise of neither man, the task seemed virtually impossible to execute successfully.

Next, McIntyre lay on the balcony deck, making himself as unresponsive as possible. From a sitting position Lewis found it impossible to lift him more than a few inches and would have had no chance of getting him over the rail from that position. Of course, there was a substantial difference in height and build between McIntyre and Anne but both men concluded it would have been extremely difficult for Dean to have disposed of his wife's body in this way, had that been his intention.

Returning inside, McIntyre pointed out the expensive clothing to Lewis, the provenance of which was now becoming much clearer following the revelation of Anne's apparent theft from her employers.

A further thorough search of the stateroom yielded nothing of interest until they came to the bathroom. Inside a small floral washbag which they assumed belonged to Anne, Lewis found four small, plastic zip-lock bags containing white powder. These bags were very similar to the ones found during the search of Andrews' cabin. The content of the bags did not appear in doubt, but they would be tested for cocaine nonetheless. Also in the washbag were a dozen white tablets identical in size and design to the ones found with Andrews and which he had identified as diazepam.

'Looks like the evidence is stacking up against Andrews as being a supplier as well as a user,' said McIntyre as Lewis handed the packages and loose tablets over to him.

'We've got quite a lot to put to Lee when we next speak to him.'

At that point, they concluded the search, ensuring that the stateroom was re-sealed and started to make their way back down to the security office.

15

'Since it's going to be a long day, fancy a spot of lunch up in the buffet restaurant?' McIntyre volunteered.

Lewis readily agreed. McIntyre quite liked the informality of the buffet, which served exactly the same food as the more formal restaurants, but in more relaxed surroundings. As it was a sea day, the buffet was extremely crowded, but they found a quiet table in a corner, where most of the officers tended to congregate.

Lewis had skipped breakfast, as he had been engrossed in Anne's diary from the moment he got up, until he went to deliver his lecture. He relished his visit to the carvery, which was serving a particularly appetising looking beef roast, completing the dish with a generously portioned selection of cooked vegetables. Normally he wouldn't have indulged in such a heavy meal this early in the day, but he knew they would probably struggle to find time to eat later on.

McIntyre, by comparison went for a lighter salad, partly because he had seen the dessert station. Having an extremely sweet tooth, he fully intended to pay it a visit to finish his meal. Both men ate in comparative silence, as they were enjoying the food on offer and also did not wish to be overheard by the other diners who were in close proximity.

Cruise ships were a hotbed of gossip, particularly amongst the crew, officers included and divulging any confidence which could be overheard was best avoided.

As they ate, Lewis casually observed his fellow diners. He was familiar with the dining etiquette, or rather lack of it, constantly on display in the buffet. There was something about being able to help oneself that seemed to bring out the glutton in so many of the passengers.

Plates were piled high with more food than a normal person could possibly eat, apparently just because it was there and presumably because they felt they had paid for it. He guessed the amount of waste in this restaurant must be staggering.

The concept of queueing also seemed to be alien to most, as the hungry hordes vied for what they considered to be the choicest portions. The buffet was constantly re-stocked, but many of the passengers still approached it as though it was about to run out of food at any moment.

Having finished their meal, the pair then strolled to the open-air seating area at the rear of the buffet, by the ship's stern. Here they could speak freely if they wanted to, without being overheard. The strong westerly wind blew the smoke from the ship's funnel almost horizontally above them, before it disappeared over the stern and merged in the distance with the churning white wakes caused by the twin propellers. They sat in contemplative silence for a few minutes, enjoying the bracing air and clearing their heads for the busy afternoon ahead.

'I think we're both agreed that we need to speak to Dean, Craig and Lee again in light of what we now know,' said McIntyre, finally breaking the silence. 'Shall we do it in that order?'

Lewis nodded his agreement, whilst McIntyre contacted his

control room to enquire if Dean had already been spotted that day. The security department had been tasked with keeping a discreet watch on both Dean and Craig Leonard, but more particularly Dean, because of his physical vulnerability and proclivity for over-imbibing.

The response came back that he had not been spotted outside of his stateroom so far during the course of the day. Having made their way to his stateroom, McIntyre knocked loudly and waited. Receiving no response, he knocked again and pressed his ear to the door and listened. Certain he could hear the sound of voices coming from inside, he knocked again and called out loudly.

'Dean, it's Calum McIntyre, security, alright if we come in?'

Again, receiving no audible reply, McIntyre opened the door using his master key and they stepped into the stateroom. As they entered, they could see that the room was in a state of disarray, with clothing strewn everywhere. Dean lay on top of the bed dressed only in a pair of shorts and a rather grubby tee-shirt. His wheelchair sat to one side of the bed.

Dressed like this and fully stretched out on the bed, both men noticed the contrast between the upper and lower halves of his body. His torso was bulky and well defined, whilst his legs were thin and spindly, the muscles wasted through lack of use. At first, Dean barely acknowledged their presence, but he slowly came to and struggled to sit upright.

'Here, let me give you a hand,' McIntyre volunteered, moving to the side of the bed ready to assist.

'It's alright, I'll manage on my own,' said Dean tetchily, apparently less than pleased at having been disturbed.

It was obvious that Dean had not shaved for at least a couple of days, as an untidy stubble covered his chin. Even allowing for the fact he had apparently just been woken, his overall appearance gave the impression of neglect, which annoyed McIntyre slightly as he had asked the sick bay staff to keep an eye on him.

Several bottles of what appeared to be prescription medication sat on one of the bedside tables and lying on the floor behind his wheelchair, McIntyre noticed a vodka bottle which was almost three-quarters empty. How Dean had managed to come by this was something of a mystery, as passengers were not permitted to bring their own alcohol on board this particular cruise line, with the exception of a couple of bottles of wine on embarkation. Of course, many passengers flouted the regulations and, particularly if they were seasoned cruisers, devised ever more ingenious ways to circumvent the prohibition.

After much effort, during which he made it clear that he required no assistance from anyone, Dean got himself into a sitting position on his bed and gradually eased himself into his wheelchair.

'I was wondering when I'd see you two again,' he said morosely, rubbing the sleep from his bloodshot eyes. 'Have you got any news for me?'

McIntyre responded. 'Nothing positive I'm afraid, but there are a few more questions we'd like to ask you. We've been doing a bit of digging and there's a few surprises that have come to light concerning your wife, which we'd like to discuss with you. You may find some of our questions a little intrusive and distressing, but I'd like you to be as open and honest as you can. So, is it ok if we just have a chat right here, to save you having to get dressed, or maybe you'd like a change of scenery?'

'Here's ok thanks. I'm not in the mood for going out at the

moment. I just want to be on my own. Some cruise this has turned out to be. I was really looking forward to it but it's turned into an absolute fucking disaster.'

At that point, Dean wore the expression of a man who had all but given up on life. There seemed to be little doubt in McIntyre and Lewis's minds that his wife's mysterious disappearance had hit him hard, emotionally and physically.

Lewis sat down at the desk at the foot of the bed, notebook and pen at the ready, whilst McIntyre made himself comfortable on the small settee on the opposite side of the bed from Dean.

'Would you like us to make you a coffee or something before we begin?' Lewis asked sympathetically, sensing that Dean needed something to liven himself up.

'Yeah, black, no sugar. I've got a throat like the bottom of a parrot's cage at the moment.'

A couple of minutes later, coffee in hand, Dean gradually became more alert and McIntyre sensed they were ready to proceed.

'Just to recap,' McIntyre began, taking the lead role. 'I think this is the third time we've spoken to you. When we first spoke a couple of days ago you told us you thought Anne was under a lot of stress, particularly at work, although she was reluctant to take time off. You also told us she was in charge of the accounts at the company. Did she ever discuss work with you at home?'.

'Not really. If I'm honest, I probably didn't show much interest in any case, but even on the few occasions that I did, she just clammed up whenever work was mentioned.'

'What I'm going to say to you now may or may not come as a

surprise. There were certain items of correspondence, including bank statements, diaries and the like which we found amongst your wife's possessions. I apologise for having had to examine them, but we really need to understand what may have happened to her and that seemed to be the most obvious place to start. Are you ready for this?'

Dean gazed across the bed, with the forlorn look of a man about to receive news he didn't want to hear.

'Would I be right in thinking that Anne was in charge of the finances for both of you?'

'Yeah, I left all that to her. It started really when I had my scaffolding business and she did the company accounts 'cos that's what she does for a living at the end of the day.'

'So how much do you know about your household bills, like your mortgage payments etc?'

'Not a lot to tell you the truth. I know the mortgage is fairly high, particularly since we moved to our present house, but I couldn't put a figure on it. Anne's very good with the finances and everything just seems to get paid. I never have to worry about any of that stuff. That's why I'm not bothered about the account being in her name only. Most couples probably have a joint bank account, but my only contribution to the household finances these days is my disability benefit, which doesn't amount to much.'

'Do you know how much she earns per month at Ace Valves?'

'No idea, but I think she's on a pretty good salary.'

'If I told you her monthly take home pay from work is two and a half thousand a month would that surprise you?'

'It would actually,' said Dean, a startled look flitting across his face. 'I thought it would be a lot more than that.'

'And your monthly mortgage payments alone come to about a thousand pounds. Doesn't leave an awful lot left to live on. In fact, from the bank statements I've seen, the outgoings from your household exceed the income from your wife's work. However, this is offset by a regular monthly payment of five thousand pounds from another account into her current account. Any idea where that money comes from?'

Dean buried his head in his hands and shook it from side to side.

'Jesus Christ, every time I see you guys you hit me with another bombshell. First it was the two other passengers who she appears to have paid for and who I don't have a fucking clue who they are and now this. What are you trying to tell me?'

'We'll come back to the other two passengers presently, but in the meantime what I'm suggesting, from the evidence we've uncovered so far, is that your wife may have had her fingers in the till at work, so to speak. What are your thoughts on that?'

Both men watched Dean very carefully for his reaction to this latest, potentially devastating revelation. There were a couple of possible scenarios they were considering. The first was that Dean would be totally unaware of any details about their domestic finances, which in fact he had already indicated. The second was that he did have some knowledge of where the money was coming from but, if it was in any way illegal, he may decide to neither confirm nor deny it, to avoid incriminating either himself or his wife.

The colour had drained completely from Dean's already pallid features. All McIntyre's training had taught him not to get emotionally involved during interview situations, but he found it very difficult to refrain from reaching out to Dean. Instead, he remained completely silent for a couple of minutes, gauging his reaction.

It seemed to McIntyre that Dean was an open book. If he was not surprised by what he had just heard, he must be a very accomplished actor, he concluded.

'Obviously we don't know too much about your personal circumstances, but we do know you've been on several other cruises with this company before and judging by the designer clothing in your stateroom, the evidence from the bank statements I've just mentioned and the fact Anne appears to have paid for an extra couple of passengers on this particular cruise, I'd say you are definitely living beyond your means as a couple. I'm afraid to say that everything points to Anne having been defrauding her employer, probably over the course of the past few years from what we've seen.'

Silent tears began to trickle down Dean's face as he stared blankly over McIntyre's shoulder. Soon, he was convulsed in sobs which seemed to come from the very pit of his stomach. His abject misery at that point was clear to see. He grabbed the duvet from the bed and buried his face in it, whilst he continued with his loud, racking sobs.

McIntyre had yet to ask him about his wife's lover and their suspicion that she was an illicit drug user and that her supplier may also be on board, paid for by her. However, at that point it seemed that Dean needed time to compose himself.

McIntyre and Lewis resisted the urge to show too much compassion, as their interviewee was still a potential suspect in his wife's disappearance and under a little bit more pressure, he may yet reveal details which would help solve the mystery.

'Tell you what Dean, I think we'll take a break for a few minutes so that you can get yourself together. I realise this has probably come as a bit of a shock to you, but unfortunately we have some more questions to put to you which you might find equally upsetting.'

Whilst Lewis remained with Dean, McIntyre left the state-room and made his way down to the sick bay. He was anxious to know whether Dean had been medically supervised over the course of the past couple of days as he had requested and wanted to arrange for one of the medical staff to certify that he was fit to continue with their interview.

Whilst he was waiting for this to be arranged, he dropped by his office, as he was conscious that the investigation was occupying what might seem to be a disproportionate amount of time to some of his staff.

As he entered, he surprised two of his security officers who appeared to be having an animated and it seemed, very heated conversation. Both were Nepalis, as were the majority of the security officers, recruited mainly because they had served as Gurkha soldiers in either the British or Indian Armies. They were speaking in what he vaguely recognised as their native language, Gorkhali, so he was unable to glean the gist of their conversation, but they stopped as soon as he entered.

The most senior of the two, Kai Rana, remained in the room, whilst the other officer, Bahadur Gurung left swiftly. As he exited the room, McIntyre noticed the latter appeared to be close to tears. This surprised him, as in his experience, the ex-Gurkhas were very reserved and private individuals and rarely showed any flicker of emotion.

'Is there a problem, Kai?' McIntyre asked, not really expecting a definitive response, as he knew the Nepalis tended to deal with any issues of concern between themselves.

'He's been acting a bit strange for the past couple of days but he refuses to tell me what the problem is. I can't help him if he won't tell me what's wrong, but I'll get to the bottom of it, don't worry guruji.'

'Ok, but if there's anything I need to know, make sure you keep me informed.'

In normal circumstances, McIntyre would have spoken to Bahadur Gurung in person, but right now he was too busy.

16

McIntyre returned to Dean Ebsworth's stateroom just as one of the ship's nurses was leaving. Dawn, a bubbly Australian, was someone McIntyre knew fairly well as she liked to socialise in the crew bar when off duty. He knew she would give him a quick and honest assessment of Dean's mental state, without overly concerning herself with patient confidentiality.

He quickly appraised her of the fact that Dean was in the process of being interviewed about the circumstances of his wife's disappearance and the interview was likely to be potentially traumatic. Dawn assured him that although Dean was obviously tearful and upset, she could confirm he had been taking all his prescribed medication over the past couple of days and had been seen by her personally on at least a couple of occasions. In her opinion, there was no reason why the interview couldn't continue.

Entering the stateroom once again, McIntyre was relieved to see Dean appeared to have regained his composure. As he resumed his seat across the bed from Dean, he caught the eye of Lewis, who gave him a reassuring wink and a discreet thumbs up.

'Right Dean. I've just had a quick word with the nurse outside and she tells me you seem to be ok to carry on with our chat. If it's alright with you I'll just take up from where we left off a few minutes ago?'

'Yeah, fine. Sorry about earlier but I'm really missing her you know.'

'Perfectly understandable mate. Now like I said before, there's a couple of other issues which we want to put to you which you may find distressing, but we have to clear them up. During our second conversation with you yesterday morning we told you Anne had paid for two other people to come on this cruise and we showed you the invoice with their names on. Do you remember that?'

'Yeah, but just remind me of the names again.'

'Craig Leonard and Lee Andrews.'

'That's right. I've been racking my brains since you showed me that invoice and I honestly can't say I've ever heard of either of them.'

'Let's deal with them one at a time then, shall we? We'll start with Craig Leonard. He lives about ten miles from your place and he works as a fitness instructor and personal trainer. We believe he works at the same gym that Anne belongs to. Bearing that in mind, are you now able to recall her ever mentioning anyone of that name?'

Dean sighed deeply as his head slumped forward towards his chest. It seemed he had quickly sensed the direction in which this line of questioning was going.

'I've never heard her mention that name. I hope I'm wrong, but I think the next thing you're going to tell me is that my wife's been having an affair with him?'

Dean looked almost pleadingly at McIntyre, hoping his

response would ease his rising anguish.

'Unfortunately, that's exactly what it looks like, Dean. Sorry to have to tell you. In fact, we've already spoken to Leonard and he's confirmed they did in fact meet at the gym about a year ago and they've been having an affair. That appears to be the reason why he's here. I'm not sure how she thought she could get away with having him on board, but presumably because of your mobility issues and the fact you've never met him, she maybe thought she could get away with inviting him along and not being found out.'

Dean was silent for a few moments and McIntyre was surprised he hadn't shown more of a reaction, particularly in light of his previous distress at the revelation that Anne may have been stealing from her employers.

'I just had a feeling that something like this would happen eventually,' he said calmly. 'Things haven't been happening in the bedroom department, so to speak and I've told her more than once that if she wanted to leave me she could, but she always said that wasn't what she wanted. If anything, I thought she might take up with someone from work, but looking back on it now, she always seemed very keen to go to the gym, particularly in the last few months.'

'So, this hasn't come as a major surprise to you?'

'No, the only surprise is that it's taken her so long. I suppose I should be grateful for that.'

Encouraged by Dean's lack of demonstrable grief or anger at this latest revelation about his wife's infidelity, McIntyre pressed on.

'Now we come to the other guy, Lee Andrews. Again, I'm asking you to think very carefully. Have you ever heard of him, or have you any idea why he should have been invited along?'

'No, like I've already told you, I'd never heard of either of those two blokes before, but go on, hit me with it, he's a former boyfriend, or long-lost brother, or something?'

'If only,' said McIntyre. 'It appears to be a little bit more complicated than that. We've also spoken to Andrews and for what it's worth, we have him locked up at the moment.'

On hearing this, Dean's eyebrows shot up and he leaned forward attentively in his wheelchair.

'You don't mean to tell me he's got something to do with her going missing?' he said, almost pleadingly.

'Well, we have no direct evidence of that, but first let me tell you something about our Mr Andrews. He's a fairly youngish guy, late twenties I believe. Lives in the same town as you and he told us he got to know Anne when he used to work at Ace Valves. He's left there now, but it appears they've kept in touch. He says he recognises you from having seen you around town, but he doesn't think you'd recognise him. Still doesn't ring a bell?'

'No, not at all, but why's he here, what's he done, why have you got him locked up?'

The words tumbled from Dean's mouth, partly, McIntyre felt, through anticipation of hearing what Andrews may have been up to and partly through fear of what the next revelation was going to be.

'When we asked him why he'd been invited along, he told us how he met Anne and he spun us a yarn about always having wanted to go on a cruise. According to him, she said he could come along on this one, which she would pay for and he could pay her back later. Do you believe that?

'Sounds like a load of old bollocks if you ask me.'

'Couldn't have put it better myself, Dean. Anyway, it's pretty obvious, without going into detail, that Lee has a serious drug problem. That's basically why we have him in custody at the moment.'

'Do you have cells on cruise ships then, or is he locked up in his cabin?' Dean asked, apparently genuinely curious.

'For obvious reasons, we don't advertise the fact, but yes, we do have the facilities to keep people in custody should the need arise,' McIntyre replied, without going into more detail.

'So, I still don't understand exactly what he's done or what this has to do with Anne going missing, apart from what you've just told me about them knowing each other from work.'

'When we searched his cabin, obviously to make sure Anne wasn't there, we found a quantity of drugs. He told us that they were for his own use as a registered heroin addict. Now this is where the jigsaw begins to fit. When we went through your original stateroom, we found what appears to be cocaine and some tablets which we think are diazepam in Anne's washbag. The substance we believe to be cocaine was in identical packaging to a similar substance found in Andrews' room. Are you beginning to get my drift?'

If Dean had shown no emotion at being told that Anne had been having an affair, this seemed to hit him like a hammer blow. How much more bad news could he take, McIntyre wondered. He remained speechless, waiting for McIntyre to spill out the awful truth which was slowly dawning on him.

'There's no easy way of putting this Dean. It seems that in

addition to her other problems and possibly because of them, Anne has been taking drugs and it appears Andrews may be her supplier. That would explain why he's on board. Not sure why he couldn't have supplied her before she left to come on the cruise, but maybe he just talked her into bringing him along. There's also references in her diary which would indicate her use of drugs, so our suspicions come from two different sources.'

'The little bastard,' Dean hissed through clenched teeth, his hands gripping the sides of his wheelchair so tightly his knuckles turned almost white. 'Good job you've got the fucker locked up, otherwise I'd track him down and kill him, I swear.'

'Well, I can assure you he's in a whole lot of trouble right now and he'll be dealt with in the right way eventually. Did you have any idea at all Anne may have been taking drugs?'

'The only thing I'm not surprised about is her taking up with this- what's his name, Leonard bloke. As to her having her fingers in the till as you put it and now taking drugs, I'm totally gobsmacked. It's like a bad dream. Please tell me there's nothing else you're going to hit me with?'

'I realise this is very difficult for you Dean and I'm sorry to be the bearer of such bad news, but you had to know. The only thing we have to try to do now is to find out what has happened to Anne. I'll be totally honest with you, when we investigate something like this, we always assume that the other half could be involved, because statistically that's how it pans out. So, I'll ask you a straightforward question. Are you in any way involved with your wife's disappearance?'

Dean stared straight ahead, all emotion already drained from his face. His reply was brief, emphatic and, it appeared, genuine.

'No.'

'One last thing whilst we're on the subject of Andrews,' McIntyre continued, 'When we spoke to him, we noticed he had some quite nasty facial injuries, which appeared recent. He gave us a reason as to how he had sustained those injuries, which may or may not be true.'

'I hope somebody gave the little bastard a good hiding,' Dean almost snarled.

'As a matter of fact, that's what it looked like. I notice you called him little just then. I don't think I've mentioned anything so far about his physical appearance. Why did you say that, are you absolutely certain you don't know him?'

'Most of these druggies are weedy little fuckers. I'm just assuming he's one of them, that's why I said it.'

'You won't mind if we have a quick look at your hands, just to satisfy ourselves you don't have any bruised knuckles or anything?' McIntyre said, more as an order than a request.

Dean readily stretched out his hands for examination. They appeared free from any signs of injury. Whilst this proved nothing, it did tend to indicate Dean had not recently been involved in any acts of violence, either directed towards his wife or Andrews.

'Anything you want to ask before we wrap up here, Mike?' McIntyre asked, looking across at Lewis.

Lewis shook his head.

'Are you going to be ok on your own here for the time being?' McIntyre asked Dean.

'Yeah, to be honest I just want a little time on my own to get to grips with what you've just told me. Despite everything, all I want right now is for Anne to walk back in through that door. It's beginning to look like that's not going to happen though, is it?'

'We're doing everything we possibly can to find her and you'll be the first to know. In the meantime, we're going to speak to Leonard and Andrews again, now we know a little bit more about their connections to Anne.'

McIntyre and Lewis then left the stateroom and made their way back to the security complex.

'Well,' McIntyre began, as they settled into his cramped office, 'Have you any more thoughts on Dean, now that we've had another chat with him?'

'I think the guy's pretty genuine. I don't think he had the faintest idea about what his wife's been up to, probably because he's been too absorbed in his own problems, which is understandable to an extent. If he didn't know about her activities, he would have no real reason to wish her any harm. I'm much more inclined to think he's got nothing to do with her disappearance than I did when we previously spoke to him.'

'I'm pretty much of the same opinion,' agreed McIntyre. 'Moving swiftly on, as they say, I suggest we speak to Leonard again next. With Andrews being banged up, he can wait.'

'Roger that,' Lewis concluded.

17

For the best part of three days now, McIntyre had been almost solely pre-occupied with the search for Anne Ebsworth. In the meantime, a myriad of outstanding matters had been building up requiring his urgent attention. Also, he was aware Lewis was being given little time to prepare his lectures and to have some down time, simply to enjoy the cruise. He knew his friend wouldn't mind, but nevertheless he felt guilty.

After voicing his thoughts to Lewis, it was agreed they would defer speaking to Leonard or Andrews until later in the evening, after they'd both had a few hours to catch up with their respective issues.

Lewis still hadn't finished reading Anne's diary and decided to spend a bit of time doing so before they resumed the interviews, but first he decided to stretch his legs and have a walk round the ship. Without McIntyre, he had to remain in the passenger areas and once again, having experienced the bland and somewhat austere surroundings of the crew quarters, he was struck by the brash opulence he encountered at every turn.

Emerging from the lift on Deck 14, he exited through a set of automatic double doors onto the open deck. He was immediately buffeted by the strength of the wind, which had picked up considerably since he had last ventured outside just after lunch. Even this high up, he could feel the light flecks of sea-spray on his face as he leant into the breeze.

Despite the conditions and the fading light, he was surprised to see a steady stream of runners and walkers using the marked, anti-slip circuit which looped around the deck. Some were couples walking briskly arm in arm, well wrapped up against the elements, whilst others appeared to be more committed solo runners, seriously intent on completing their target times or number of circuits.

Lewis ventured even higher up a steep flight of steps towards the front of the vessel, which took him to Deck 15, the highest point on the ship which could be accessed by passengers. The multipurpose games court, surrounded by high netting, lay empty. A couple of footballs which had been left out on the court rolled backwards and forwards over its surface, moving with the motion of the ship and the force of the wind which was now blowing directly onto the ship's bow. The open area outside the games court which would normally be used by sunbathers lay empty, all the deckchairs firmly lashed to the bulkheads.

Lewis had to struggle forward to reach the rail at the front of the deck as the wind at this height was so fierce it threatened to blow him backwards. He was not surprised to find he was alone.

Despite the wind chill which made the temperature seem much colder than it actually was, Lewis remained by the rail for at least ten minutes. There was something almost hypnotic about the motion of the ship as the bow plunged down into the white tipped waves, causing spray to break over the railings, before rising again to power its way forward through the vast emptiness of the ocean. In the gloom of the approaching dusk, Lewis felt alone but strangely at peace. He needed this time to clear his head and mull over the events of the last few days.

Anne was missing and they were no nearer to finding out what had happened to her. Normally by this stage of an investigation, an obvious suspect would have emerged, but this case was rather more perplexing.

The crime scene, if there was one, could be anywhere on the ship, making their task even more difficult. Lost in thought, Lewis was finally compelled to abandon his lofty perch by the biting wind, which was by now beginning to chill him to the bone.

As he descended from Deck 15, Lewis re-entered a different world. Suddenly he was back amidst the bustle of shipboard life, but his time alone had cleared his head and he felt re-energized. For some unknown reason he was drawn to Deck 10, where he found himself outside stateroom 1249, which still bore its *Do Not Enter* sticker on the door.

As he stood outside, he tried to imagine the scene just over three days earlier, when Anne had walked out of that door for the last time. What was she thinking at that precise moment? There were many issues going on in her life which could cause her distress, yet only a few minutes later she would be seen on CCTV apparently happy in the company of her lover, Craig Leonard. She hadn't been seen since however and it now seemed clear to Lewis that Leonard was becoming a person of significant interest in the investigation.

Returning to his stateroom, Lewis ordered a light supper via room service and settled down to read some more extracts from Anne's diary.

Around nine o'clock, he was joined by McIntyre, who had used the last few hours to deal with his various other duties as head of the security department. He advised Lewis that on his way up, he had dropped past Leonard's stateroom but had received no response. The cabin steward hadn't seen him for several hours and McIntyre had also checked the gym but he wasn't there.

A decision was made to interview Andrews next as he was readily available in the brig and Leonard could be revisited the following morning when it would be easier to find him. Back in the security office, McIntyre unlocked the brig and shook the slumbering form of Andrews into consciousness.

Andrews had been locked up now for just over twenty-four hours and McIntyre wasn't sure what he would find. When he had seen him earlier in the day, Andrews had been in full cold turkey mode. In his experience, drug addicts didn't usually react well to being incarcerated, particularly in the early stages and usually exhibited fairly extreme withdrawal symptoms. This could range from acute paranoia to profuse sweating, anxiety and sometimes extreme aggression. Andrews, however now showed none of those signs and appeared remarkably docile, even a little subdued. McIntyre guessed the fact he was being allowed to carry on with his methadone prescription was at least keeping him stable. He guided the slightly unsteady young man the short distance to the interview room, where Lewis was already waiting and motioned for him to sit down at the far side of the small desk, furthest from the door.

'Evening, young man,' Lewis said airily, as he took his seat.

Andrews merely grunted, not yet fully awake. He rubbed the sleep from his bloodshot eyes and licked his dry lips.

'How are you feeling now, Lee?' McIntyre continued. 'Being well looked after I hope?'

'Better still if I wasn't here but I've just got to make the best of it. Are you going to let me go soon? Obviously, I shouldn't have brought drugs on to the ship, but you've got them all now, so I don't see the point in keeping me banged up,' Andrews' voice sounded croaky. 'I'm a bit parched, any chance of a glass of water?'

'Of course,' Lewis replied, filling a plastic cup from a cold-water dispenser and handing it to the young man.

'Right,' said McIntyre, settling into a seat on the opposite side of the desk from Andrews. 'When we spoke to you last night, we discovered quite a little stash of drugs in your cabin. Coke, crack cocaine, methadone and, you say, diazepam. We also found a couple of crack pipes. Are you still maintaining all those substances were for your own personal use?'

'I can hardly deny it, can I?'

'That's not exactly what I asked,' pressed McIntyre. 'What I'm trying to figure out is whether they were for your own use, or maybe you've been dealing whilst on the ship?'

'Leave it out, do I look like a dealer to you?'

'If I knew the answer to that question, I'd be the best ship security officer at sea. Seems like an awful lot of drugs just for yourself. If you're saying that's the case, then you must have a very serious habit.'

'I've already told you I'm a recovering heroin addict and the methadone and benzos are mine; I've got a script for them. OK, I shouldn't be using the cocaine, but it's not easy you know, coming off the gear.'

'Even so, it's stretching it a bit to ask me to believe that you'd get through the quantity of drugs we found, in two weeks.'

Andrews shrugged his shoulders and stretched his arms out wide, his open palms facing forward.

'Let me help you out a bit here Lee,' McIntyre continued. 'The reason why you ended up here in the first place is because you know Anne Ebsworth, correct?'

'Yeah, I suppose.'

'You told us how you came to know her and why she had paid for you to come on this cruise, again correct?'

'Yeah,' replied Andrews warily, wondering where this line of questioning was leading to.

'And correct me if I'm wrong, but you said the last time you saw her was on Monday afternoon, right?'

'That's what I said, what day is it today by the way?' replied Andrews, who appeared to have genuinely lost track of time.

'Friday. Now, during our search for Anne we've come up with some good evidence to show she's has been taking drugs, specifically coke and diazepam or benzos as you call them. She kept a diary which gives details of meetings with her supplier and exactly what she was buying.'

Although the diary entries were by no means conclusive proof that Andrews was her supplier, McIntyre wasn't going to reveal that to him at this point and hoped his bluff would elicit a damning response.

Andrews remained silent.

'Did you introduce Anne to drugs, or did she come to you, probably as someone she knew who used them?' McIntyre persevered.

Again, Andrews didn't answer.

'Look Lee, you really want to start thinking about

co-operating here, because whether you realise it or not, you're in deep trouble. We've got you bang to rights for being in possession of controlled drugs on board this ship. That's just as serious as if you'd been caught with them ashore. In your case however, it's even worse, because to all intents and purposes, this ship is American territory.'

'How do you figure that out?' queried Andrews, finally breaking his silence.

'Simple. It's an American registered ship and the next port of call is in the US. When we found the drugs in your possession, we were in international waters. The Yanks will be dealing with you when we get to New York, which is our first stop. Mark my words, there's no way you'll be seeing the Caribbean. More likely the inside of a New York jail, which I don't imagine is a very pleasant prospect.'

'They'll probably just bang me up for a couple of days, then deport me,' replied Andrews casually, apparently not quite grasping the significance of what he had just been told.

'It doesn't work like that, take it from me,' McIntyre went on. 'I had a similar case last year, without the added complication of a missing person being thrown in and the guy concerned is currently doing a seven to ten-year stretch. He was also taken off the ship at New York and spent some time on Rikers Island before being transferred to a Federal jail which is probably lucky for him. I don't know if you've ever heard of Rikers Island, but it's supposed to be one of the top ten worst jails in America.'

McIntyre now had Andrews' undivided attention. His whole demeanour changed in an instant, the seriousness of his predicament having been spelt out to him. His soporific gaze became one of startled alertness. McIntyre sensed it was time to go for the jugular.

'Believe me, they do things differently in America. The way they'll probably look at it is, if you hadn't been caught, you could have come ashore with all those drugs in your possession and they're likely to be less than lenient. Given the amount we found on you, I reckon you could be looking at up to ten years at the very least.'

Andrews already pasty features had by now turned ashen. The gravity of his position was beginning to register.

'I'm not sure how you'd survive in an American prison, Lee,' continued McIntyre, ramping up the pressure. 'Imagine not seeing England again for at least the next ten years. Pretty scary thought don't you think?'

'What do you want me to say?' replied Andrews, a look of panic now etched on his face.

'All I want you to do is to tell us the truth, then maybe we can give you a bit of a leg up. I'm not promising anything at the moment, but if you help us, we can say to the Americans you've been co-operative and that can only do you good. At the moment we're having to drag everything out of you and I wouldn't say you're being very helpful at all.'

'Go on then,' said Andrews expectantly.

'Let's break this down. Did you know Anne was taking drugs?'

After a slight hesitation, Andrews answered.

'Yeah.'

'How long have you known?'

'Are you sure you're going to help me out if I level with you?' asked Andrews, shifting uncomfortably in his seat.

'We'll do our very best, I promise. I've got no great desire to see you waste the next few years of your life in an American jail,' replied McIntyre, sensing a breakthrough.

'The reason I left Ace Valves where we both worked, was we were all given a random drugs test one day. They did that sometimes because we worked with precision machinery. Back then I'd only just started using heroin and I didn't really have a problem with it, but of course it showed up in the test. The result was I was fired on the spot.

I went on a bit of a downhill spiral after that and looking back on it, that was probably the start of my addiction. Obviously being fairly high up in the company, Anne knew exactly what had happened. Anyhow I never had any more to do with her for a long time, but I did occasionally bump into her around town now and again and to be fair, she was always ok with me, although I think she knew I was still on the gear,' Andrews paused.

'Go on.'

'Well one day a few months back I was in the town centre one Saturday afternoon and we bumped into each other. We just sort of exchanged pleasantries as you do, then she asked me if I fancied going for a coffee. I was a bit surprised to tell you the truth, but I went along with her because I've always found her to be quite a nice person actually. Whilst we were having coffee, she asked me outright if I was still taking drugs, although I guess it was pretty obvious to her what the answer was. I didn't see much point in denying it, so I told her I was, but I was trying to get clean.'

Andrews paused again. He was beginning to open up, but still needed some prompting.

'Then what?'

'We had a bit of a general chat and we ended up speaking about Ace Valves. I told her I had enjoyed my time working there and how much I regretted losing my job. Even though I was taking a little bit of heroin at that time, I probably wouldn't have ended up in the mess I'm in now if I'd been kept on.

She said she sympathised with my predicament and was sorry I'd been fired, but there was nothing she could have done about it. I told her I understood and didn't blame her in the slightest. She told me she was under a lot of pressure at work herself and was also struggling to deal with her domestic situation, which obviously I knew about and much to my surprise, she almost broke down in tears, right there in front of me.'

'What did you think about that?'

'I was really surprised if I'm honest. I'm more used to pouring my problems out to other people, but suddenly here I was listening. It was strange, but I actually felt very sorry for her. I could see that she was under a lot of pressure and I suddenly realised why she had asked me to have coffee with her.'

'I'm listening,' said McIntyre, not wishing to interrupt the flow.

'Most of the conversation was about drugs actually, then she just came straight out with it. She asked me what it was like to take cocaine and I just described to her how it felt to me. I didn't tell her I used crack, but I said that the coke gave me a buzz and helped me forget my problems for a short while at least. She said she fancied trying it. I was a bit taken aback to be truthful and I didn't think she was being serious, but I said I could get her a sample to try out if that's what she really wanted. We exchanged phone numbers and I met her a few days later. I gave her a gram bag to try out.'

'How much did you charge her for that?'

'Forty-five quid. I didn't make any profit on that at all, as that's more or less what I was paying for it myself, but I was sort of doing her a favour.'

'And maybe doing yourself a favour as well, as that's a common ploy, to start them off cheap until they become regulars,' suggested McIntyre.

'No, that wasn't my intention at all,' Andrews interjected, seemingly annoyed at the suggestion.

'I thought she'd probably just try it and she'd never ask again. At that time, I didn't think she'd become a regular user, because she just didn't seem the type. After I'd handed it over, I even had to tell her how to cut it into lines and show her how to snort it. I even used some of my own gear to do the demo,' he added, as if it was an act of great chivalry.

'So how did it go after that?'

'Just over a week later, she got in touch with me again and asked me for another gram. She told me that she'd been doing a line a day, which would have been about right, as you normally get about seven to ten lines out of a gram, as long as you don't go mad.'

'And this time, how much did you charge?'

'Bearing in mind I was the one taking all the risks, I upped the price to fifty- five pounds. Also, there wasn't a lot of it about at that time, so the prices were going up anyhow. I still didn't really make anything out of it.'

'So, if you weren't already, you'd now gone from being a drug user to a drug dealer?'

'I've never really considered myself to be a drug dealer. I

admit I might sell the odd small amount to mates and to people like Anne, but I only do it to fund my own habit. As you can probably see, I haven't got a pot to piss in, so if I was a big time Charlie dealer, I wouldn't be in the state I'm in now.'

'Pardon the pun,' said McIntyre.

'What?' replied Andrews, a blank expression on his face.

'You made reference to being a big time Charlie dealer. We all know what Charlie is in street slang, don't we?' teased McIntyre.

'No, that's not what I was trying to say. Look, you're trying to trip me up here.'

McIntyre could see that Andrews was beginning to sweat and become fidgety. He had checked his medication sheet before the interview commenced and was aware he was due to have his methadone administered within the next few minutes. After that, he was likely to become drowsy and unresponsive.

'I think we'll let you have your meds, then you can put your head down for the night. You're doing very well by the way. I think we're now beginning to get to the truth. We'll continue this in the morning.'

McIntyre then returned Andrews to the brig and called the duty nurse. Returning to his office he glanced at his watch. It had gone eleven o'clock.

'I'll just give the captain a quick update over the phone to keep him in the loop, then it's time to hit the crew bar again,' he said to Lewis, who nodded enthusiastically. Lewis's time up on Deck 15 a few hours previously had given him his second wind.

18

Just before midnight, both men entered the crew bar for the second time that week. This time it was even busier, as Friday was karaoke night. A space had been cleared for the karaoke machine in one corner of the bar, furthest from the doorway leading out to the open seating area, presumably so that the sound could not be heard by the passengers on the upper decks.

Many of the crew took the karaoke sessions seriously and they were eagerly anticipated. McIntyre had been pleasantly surprised by the standard of singing and it was here that unofficial auditions were held to select participants for the crew revue, which usually took place in the ship's theatre at the end of the cruise. McIntyre himself had been known to take part when the mood took him. Like many people who had been brought up in remote island communities providing their own entertainment, he was a talented singer.

As they moved through the bar towards the outside area by the stern, Lewis noticed the many nods of acknowledgment towards his colleague that he had observed the previous evening. This time however, quite a few crew members appeared to recognise him as well. This was perhaps not surprising as he had been delivering his daily lectures now for five days and he had been constantly seen in McIntyre's company.

The table they had sat at the previous evening was surprisingly unoccupied so both men sat down, just as the first participant in the karaoke took to the microphone. Talent was not a word that could be attributed to this particular performer Lewis thought, as he rolled his eyes in mock horror towards McIntyre.

'Don't worry Mike, it gets better. They usually start with someone who can't sing, as that seems to encourage the others to think they can do better. It usually works.'

'You singing tonight, Mr Mac?' called out Leroy, one of the Jamaican barmen, in his deep West Indian baritone, as he passed their table with a tray of drinks.

'No, I think I'll spare you all this time,' smiled McIntyre. 'Whilst you're here Leroy, get us a couple of dark rums, large ones naturally and a couple of Red Stripes. Put it on my tab and have one yourself.'

McIntyre knew that the rums Leroy returned with would be generously proportioned and they would both be well looked after for the rest of the evening.

Despite the fact they were sailing into the wind, they were sheltered by their position at the stern of the ship. It was still chilly out on the open deck however and Lewis was glad he had brought along a fleece, which he zipped right up to his chin. McIntyre, having also anticipated the likely conditions, had donned a windproof uniform jacket he used for his deck rounds.

For a while neither man discussed the events of the day, but instead sat back and enjoyed their drinks and the mixed attempts at talent emanating from the direction of the karaoke machine. Out here nobody bothered them and McIntyre was glad he had spotted Leroy early, as he knew that otherwise, every time he went up to the bar, he would be accosted by well-meaning crew members wishing to pass the time with him. Tonight, he was too tired and too pre-occupied with the task in hand.

They had been sitting at their table for a few minutes when McIntyre noticed one of his security officers, in full uniform, patrolling towards them through the bar area. This was not unusual, as it was part of their remit to try to curb the excesses of some of the more exuberant crew members, especially after they'd had too much to drink. As he picked his way through the throng of revellers and headed out towards their position on the open deck, McIntyre could see the officer was in fact Bahadur Gurung.

He recognised him as the officer whom he had seen in animated conversation with Kai Rana earlier the previous afternoon and who had left abruptly when he entered the office. As he stepped out on to the deck, Gurung briefly surveyed the assembled drinkers, before catching sight of Lewis and McIntyre in their slightly secluded position by the port rail.

He quickly averted his gaze as if he hadn't seen them, but McIntyre was certain he had, because for a fleeting moment their eyes met. Gurung quickly withdrew back into the bar before disappearing completely from sight.

This was very odd, McIntyre thought, as it would have been a matter of common courtesy for Gurung to have acknowledged his boss. As ex-Gurkhas, the Nepalis were extremely rank conscious and held their officers in high esteem. Clearly, something was troubling him, as the behaviour McIntyre had just witnessed was completely out of character. Momentarily, he felt a twinge of guilt that he had become so engrossed in the search for Anne, that he may have taken his eye off the ball when it came to dealing with staff welfare. He made a mental note to himself that he would speak to Gurung first thing in the morning.

'He seemed to beat a hasty retreat when he caught sight of you, Calum,' Lewis observed presciently.

'Yeah, I don't know what's going on there but I seem to have a bit of a staff problem on my hands.'

McIntyre didn't wish to burden Lewis with the details of his encounter with Gurung earlier the previous day and made no further comment.

'Just before we turn in Mike, what do you make of our latest chat with Andrews? He was definitely beginning to open up, but I could see he was beginning to flag, which was why I wrapped it up for the night.'

'Yeah, the prospect of American justice doesn't seem to appeal to him too much. I think he's beginning to think we'll do him a favour so hopefully he'll continue in the same vein in the morning.'

Before leaving the crew bar, both men agreed the day ahead was going to be full on yet again. Although neither would admit it, they were growing increasingly concerned for the fate of Anne and the likelihood of a positive outcome was becoming ever more remote it seemed. They had done everything they could so far to try to locate her, but all efforts had drawn a blank. The pending interviews with Andrews and Leonard were going to be crucial, as they both felt that neither man was being entirely truthful about the extent of their dealings with her.

McIntyre was keen to have something positive to report to the captain at morning prayers and Lewis had his usual lecture to deliver, even though it was a Saturday. Therefore, they agreed to finish speaking with Andrews before either event.

As they pushed their way through the now boisterous throng in the bar on their way to the exit, McIntyre wondered to himself whether they should be here at all, but they hadn't exactly been resting on their laurels over the past few days. They had earned a little bit of down time.

Relaxation and sleep were in short supply however, which was why, a few hours later just before seven, McIntyre was back in his office. Breakfast would have to wait, he decided, as there was too much work to be done. After receiving the report from his night duty supervisor, he asked for Bahadur Gurung to be brought to his office, so he could try to ascertain what appeared to be troubling him.

He was told that Gurung, who had been covering the night shift, was already in his cabin asleep. Since he had not been due to come off duty until seven o'clock, this surprised McIntyre, but he was informed that Gurung had requested the last hour off as he was apparently feeling unwell. Perhaps this was the explanation for his recent strange behaviour, McIntyre thought to himself.

His next port of call was the brig. Unlocking the door, he entered the confined space, which smelt distinctly of stale body odour. To his surprise, Andrews was already awake and sitting at the pillow end of his bunk, back against the wall, knees bent towards his chin. He seemed calm, but McIntyre noticed the dark circles under his eyes, as if he hadn't had much sleep.

'How are you feeling this morning, Lee?'

'Still feel a bit like shit, but I'm due my methadone script soon. Is it on its way?'

'I'll make sure it is, then if it's ok with you, we'll carry on from where we left off last night. Fancy a bit of breakfast first?'

'Nah, just a cup of coffee thanks.'

McIntyre wasn't surprised that Andrews had refused the offer of food, as his skinny frame bore testimony to his eating habits.

Returning to his office, McIntyre was joined a few minutes later by Lewis who was smartly dressed in his presenting attire, minus the bow tie and white jacket, carried in a clear plastic cover, which he hung behind the door.

'Bit over-dressed this morning, guv'nor,' teased McIntyre, using the vernacular for a senior officer, from his police days.

'I know. We're going to speak to Andrews first and I wasn't sure how long it's going to take, so I've come prepared just in case I have to go straight to my lecture from here. However, I'll go the full Monty and put on the white jacket and dickie bow if you think it'll get him to cough,' Lewis laughed, carrying on the joke.

A few minutes later, a suitably medicated Andrews had resumed his position from the previous night in the interview room, a large plastic cup of coffee clutched between his hands.

'Right, you were being very helpful when we spoke to you last night, but I think you were beginning to flag a bit, so we thought we'd give you a break,' McIntyre began, trying to maintain his interviewee's co-operation.

'You told us you had been supplying Anne with coke for a few months.'

'Yeah, but remember I also told you it was her who approached me,' Andrews interrupted testily. 'It sounds like you're trying to make me out to be some sort of low life dealer. I told you last night I only supply to friends.'

'Point taken - I accept that,' countered McIntyre, trying to keep the conversation non-confrontational. 'Now when we searched both your cabin and Anne's we also found a quantity of what appears to be diazepam tablets. The tablets we found were identical. So, would I be right in saying that in addition to the coke, you were also supplying her with the tablets?'

Andrews nodded.

'When did you start supplying her with them?'

'A couple of months or so after she started taking the coke. She said she needed something to calm her down, especially when she was at work. I'd been prescribed them myself for a while and I told her they might do the trick. I also knew a guy who could get hold of them for a price, so it just went from there.'

'How much were you charging her for the tablets?'

'Can't remember to begin with, but latterly, seventy pence each.'

'What I can't quite get my head round,' mused McIntyre, leaning back in his chair, hands clasped behind his head, 'is why she invited you along on this cruise and paid for you? If it was to keep supplying her with drugs, why didn't she just buy enough off you before she left and save herself a bit of money?'

'She's a pretty straight sort of person at heart. She knew what she was doing was illegal and she's been on cruises before. She told me security isn't nearly as tight as it is at airports, but she didn't want to risk being caught in possession. She said if I was willing to bring the drugs on board for her, she would pay for the trip and it wouldn't cost me a penny.'

'So, you agreed to that?'

'No brainer really. I knew there was a bit of risk of course, but I quite often get stopped by the old bill back home, sometimes when I've been carrying and I've never been caught. I wasn't too worried and I was getting a free holiday out of it. What's not to like?' smirked Andrews, seemingly proud he'd outwitted security when bringing the drugs on board.

'So, what was the deal once you got on board? How often were you going to meet?'

'We hadn't made any definite plans. I saw her shortly after we got on the ship at Southampton on Sunday. I think that was just so she could see I'd made it safely. Then the last time I saw her was the following day, in the afternoon, when I gave her a gram of coke and about ten benzos.'

All this time, Lewis sat at one end of the desk, quietly observing Andrews, searching for any clues in his body language to suggest that he may be lying. Occasionally he jotted a few lines in his notebook in response to a question or answer.

'When you claim you last saw her,' continued McIntyre, 'how did she seem to you?'

'A bit strung out to be honest. She didn't really seem to be having as great a time as you would expect somebody on holiday to be having.'

'Ok, so we now know why you're really here, because you're Anne's supplier. Not what you told us initially, but top marks for getting around to the truth of the matter eventually,' soothed McIntyre. 'Now one other thing. When we spoke to you before, we asked you if there was anyone else in Anne's party, apart from yourself and Dean, that is. Remind me what you told us?'

'I think I said no. Well, I must have done 'cos I'm not aware of anyone else,' Andrews replied. McIntyre noticed his posture stiffen.

McIntyre glanced at Lewis and arched his eyebrows inquisitively. Lewis seemed to understand instinctively what he meant. He turned back the pages of his notebook until he came to an entry which he studied for a few seconds.

'Yes, that's what he told us.'

'Let me show you something Lee,' continued McIntyre, sliding a copy of the cruise invoice across the desk to the young man. 'Go on, have a look.'

Andrews studied the document for a few seconds, before gulping several times and averting his interrogator's gaze. A couple of beads of sweat began to appear on his brow.

'Well,' probed McIntyre, 'what do you have to say about that?'

'Four names on there,' croaked Andrews, taking a long swig of his coffee. Too long it seemed- thinking time.

'Exactly. The fourth name is Craig Leonard. Tell me about him, Lee?'

'I've told you already. I didn't know about anyone else,' mumbled Andrews, unconvincingly.

'You've been doing pretty well up to now, but I don't think you're being entirely truthful about that. Forget about the drugs side of things for the moment and consider this. A passenger is missing. She's come on board with three men, one of whom is her husband. As things stand at the moment, any one of those three could be responsible for her disappearance and that includes you, obviously.'

'I swear to God, it's nothing to do with me. I've told you everything I know.'

'During this enquiry, we've studied a lot of CCTV footage,' said McIntyre, enigmatically. 'I'll ask you again, what do you know about Craig Leonard?'

McIntyre knew unless he could present Andrews with some sort of evidence, or proof of association, he was unlikely to admit to knowing Leonard, if indeed he did. His gut instinct told him however that the two men had already met, either before or after boarding the ship. He had discussed this possibility with Lewis prior to the interview and he was in total agreement.

Nevertheless, his remark to Andrews was a total bluff and would have been judged inadmissible in an official police interview, where complete disclosure was required before putting questions to a suspect. They were in mid-Atlantic however, dealing with an incident pointing increasingly to foul play and they weren't the police. A few mind games wouldn't go amiss.

Andrews leaned forward, elbows on the desk, his head buried in his hands. McIntyre allowed a long pause before finally breaking the silence.

'Well?'

Andrews glanced up, a look of resignation on his face.

'Ok, I have met him, but only once and thank fuck for that,' he responded, making a circular motion round his facial injuries with his right forefinger.

'Are you saying he did that?' McIntyre queried.

'Yeah, I guess I'm safe telling you. He's not going to get to me now, what with me being banged up down here.'

'Right, from the beginning, tell me exactly how you came to meet him and what happened?'

'Can't remember exactly what day it was, might have been Tuesday. Just before lunchtime. I was in my cabin, still in bed cos I'd stayed up late. There was a knock on the door. At first, I thought it was the guy who does the room, so I shouted 'yeah' or whatever, thinking he'd let himself in. The knocking carried on so I got up and opened the door. This big bald-headed geezer was standing there. He was wearing training gear as though he'd been to the gym. He looked really pumped up and to be honest I nearly shit myself,' Andrews shuddered visibly at the memory.

'Go on.'

'He asked me if I was Lee and before I could even answer, he pushed me back into the cabin. He said something along the lines of me being exactly the sort of low life junkie scum he'd expected to find.'

Tears began to well up in Andrews' eyes as he hesitated.

'Then what happened?'

'Bearing in mind I'd never seen the geezer before; I was totally shocked. At first, I thought he'd got the wrong cabin, but he'd asked if I was Lee and I suppose he got it right about me being a junkie, so I guessed he knew exactly who I was somehow.'

Again, Andrews paused, as if he was unwilling to recall what happened next.

'Carry on Lee, you're doing well.'

'I can't really remember exactly everything he said, but he told me he was a friend of Anne's and she had told him I was supplying her with drugs. He didn't even ask me if it was true or not,' said Andrews indignantly, 'He said if he found out I did it again he'd kill me. He told me he knew people on the ship who could make me disappear and no-one would ever find me again.'

'At what point did he assault you?'

'More or less as soon as he'd said he'd kill me. He said just so I could see he meant business; he was going to give me a little taster of what was to come.'

The tears began to flow as Andrews was forced to recall the memory of what happened next.

'He grabbed me by the shoulders and lifted me right off my feet. He then turned me round and slammed my head face first into the wall. He's a fucking animal,' Andrews wailed.

'Ok Lee, we're nearly done for now. Just a couple of things about this guy. Are you saying that the very first time you met him was when he came to your cabin?'

'It's the only time I've met him,' said Andrews, slowly regaining his composure.

'So before then, you knew nothing about him, not even his name?'

'Nothing at all. I didn't know his name until you showed me that piece of paper. Even now, I've already forgotten it.'

'So, the bit about you falling down the stairs was all made up?'

Andrews nodded.

'When he said he was a friend of Anne's, did he expand on that?'

'No, that's all he said.'

'And finally, when he said he knew people on the ship who could make you disappear, did he elaborate on that at all?'

Andrews shook his head.

'Again, you've been very helpful, Lee,' McIntyre said, leaning across the desk to pat the young man on the shoulder. 'In the meantime, we'll be speaking to this guy Leonard very shortly. Like you said, you're in the best place right now. He can't do you any more harm.'

A relieved Andrews was then returned to the brig.

19

Lewis left to prepare for his lecture. He drew scant attention as he strode along the I-95 towards the lift, fully resplendent in his white jacket and bow tie with a red silk rose in his buttonhole. The crew were an eclectic mix and anyone who appeared in any way out of the ordinary barely merited a second glance.

McIntyre made his way to the captain's office to attend morning prayers. The business of the day was conducted swiftly as always and finished in just over ten minutes. At the conclusion of the meeting Captain Alex asked McIntyre to stay behind, whilst everyone else left the room.

A quick update on the progress of the investigation followed. McIntyre was glad they had made an early start interviewing Andrews, as he hoped it would show to the captain they were making headway. The fact he could now prove a link between Leonard and Andrews was a positive. McIntyre sensed however, that Captain Alex was noticeably less friendly in his manner towards him than normal and he detected a certain froideur.

He couldn't quite decide why. Was it because they were less than forty-eight hours from reaching New York, with a passenger still unaccounted for? Or perhaps he had learned McIntyre and Lewis had been in the crew bar until the early hours of the morning? McIntyre had noticed a couple of senior officers do a walk-through of the bar whilst they were there and it was possible they might have reported back to the captain.

Whatever the reason, he now felt under increasing pressure to close out the investigation.

He had only been back in his office for a few minutes, when there was a knock on the door. A couple of seconds later a man whom he recognised as one of the room steward supervisors entered, closely followed by a rather frightened looking steward.

'Sorry to disturb you, sir,' said the supervisor deferentially. McIntyre noticed he had a folded tissue in his right hand, which he deposited on the desk in front of him.

'Roberto here is the steward for 6201 on Deck 6, Mr Leonard's room. Tell sir what you found,' he said, motioning towards the steward.

'I was cleaning Mr Leonard's room this morning sir. When I moved the bed, I noticed it lying on the floor,' Roberto replied, pointing to the tissue.

McIntyre carefully unfolded the tissue and saw what appeared to be a small stud earring in the form of a diamond or similar gemstone. The steward looked uncomfortable, as if he was unsure whether he had followed the correct procedure.

'You did exactly the right thing bringing this to me, Roberto,' said McIntyre, giving him a reassuring smile. 'Prior to this morning, when was the last time you cleaned under his bed?'

'Maybe a couple of days ago,' he said defensively, aware that the supervisor was listening. 'Mr Leonard is very tidy and he doesn't like me touching his things too much.'

McIntyre knew the steward would by now have become

aware of their interest in Leonard and felt he may be a valuable source of information.

'Have you ever seen Mr Leonard with the missing lady?'

Roberto shifted uneasily and glanced towards his supervisor, before clearing his throat and replying.

'She visited him in his cabin many times, almost as soon as they got on board. At first I thought she was his wife.'

'When did you last see her with him?'

'I have been thinking about that after I was told she had gone missing. I don't really remember exactly when sir, but it must be three or four days ago.'

'I'm asking you a serious question here, Roberto. I know you probably don't think it's your place to discuss the guests, but what do you think of Mr Leonard?'

Again, Roberto looked nervously at the supervisor, who gave him a commanding nod, before replying.

'I haven't spoken to him much sir. A couple of times I've gone to his room to clean, he's told me not to bother. He doesn't seem to be a very friendly gentleman.'

McIntyre sealed the earring in a clear plastic bag, which he labelled with the steward's initials, followed by the figure one to denote the exhibit number and got him to sign over the seal.

After the steward had left, McIntyre got one of his staff to play back the CCTV images showing Anne and the man whom they now knew to be Leonard, which had been taken in the buffet restaurant, on the night she had gone missing. Because of the angle of the footage and the length of Anne's hair, he was unable to see conclusively whether or not she was wearing ear studs that matched the one he had just taken possession of.

Speaking to Leonard again had now become a matter of urgency, but it would still be an hour or so until Lewis finished his lecture, so McIntyre decided to do a deck round. He normally enjoyed these, as it gave him the opportunity to mingle with the passengers, stretch his legs and get a bit of fresh air.

He decided to start from the top down so he made his way to Deck 15. Alighting from the lift, he first made his way towards the Chill Out Zone, situated at the bow of the ship, just behind the sports court. The Chill Out Zone was where the younger passengers, up to the age of about seventeen, took part in various activities, under the supervision of trained staff. On this cruise, because it was out-with the school holiday period, the area was reasonably quiet and very few youngsters were to be seen.

Making his way forward on the open deck, McIntyre noticed a group of young teenagers in the enclosed sports court, engaged in an energetic game of basketball. From their accents, he guessed they were a mixture of Brits and Americans. He marvelled at how comfortable they seemed to be in each other's company, even though they had boarded as complete strangers only a few days previously. His trained eye took in some flirtatious behaviour. There was something about the sea air and the seemingly exotic allure of someone from a different background that seemed to promote this, as he had observed on previous trips.

For a few brief minutes, McIntyre stood gazing over the railings. Although the weather was overcast and breezy, visibility was good and for the first time in several days he could actually see a number of ships to both port and starboard, a sure sign that they were approaching the busy shipping lanes of the US eastern seaboard.

He then descended the stairs to Deck 14, before climbing back up to Deck 15 at the rear of the ship. This housed an outdoor bar area, which was unsurprisingly quiet given the weather conditions and the fact it was still only mid-morning. At the rear of the bar, about half the width of the deck was covered in artificial grass. One end was laid out as a pitch and putt course, which at that moment was not in use.

At the other end, a bocce tournament between six teams of four was in progress. Bocce, a cross between the British game of bowls and the French game petanque, always seemed very popular with the passengers and today was no exception. Most of the players were middle-aged or older. He watched for a couple of minutes, listening to the variety of regional British accents, as the participants vied for victory. Declining an offer to join in, McIntyre made his way back down to Deck 14.

He grabbed a quick take away coffee from the pool bar which was open, despite the pool being deserted. He walked the length of the jogging track, which was always popular on a sea day, before reaching the Vista Lounge situated at the front of the ship. This was a large auditorium with plush seating, which afforded panoramic views of the route ahead and to either side of the ship. Many passengers came here to read or just to completely chill out.

As he entered the lounge, a group of about twenty or so passengers were undergoing a briefing before embarking on the 3As tour (Access All Areas). This took them behind the scenes, to parts of the ship that passengers wouldn't normally see, such as the navigational bridge, engine control room, kitchens and ship's laundry. At ninety dollars per head, it wasn't cheap, but the tours were always fully subscribed.

Moving into the auditorium, McIntyre could see numerous works of art propped up on easels around the room, in preparation for the art auction which was due to take place later that morning. When he first started working on cruise ships, McIntyre often wondered if anyone actually bought any of the art on display and felt the whole set up was a bit of a charade, designed to give the impression of glamour.

Subsequently however, he had befriended a couple of the onboard art auctioneers, who enjoyed the status of officers. The auctioneers were invariably larger than life characters and he was naturally drawn to them during their off-duty hours. Most of the exhibits on display were supplied by a large auction house in the United States, which would typically supply several cruise lines simultaneously.

Training to be an art auctioneer was rigorous and the drop-out rate was extremely high. Usually, after their land-based training, the aspiring auctioneers would be allocated to a ship, under the tutelage of an experienced practitioner. It was something of a lottery as to which ship or which auctioneer they were assigned to and many of the trainees did not have their contracts renewed, as a consequence of not achieving their sales targets, or simply not getting on with their mentor.

Initially, the salary was barely enough to cover their living expenses, but with commission, some of the more experienced auctioneers earned a very good living. The constant battle to reach their sales targets took its toll however and McIntyre generally found that after a couple of years, the auctioneers whom he had spent time with left for pastures new, broken by alcoholism, stress or both.

As he prepared to walk out of the Vista Lounge, the morning quiz was just about to commence, under the direction of Rolf, a flamboyant South African. The quiz was very well attended and from the repartee he heard between Rolf and the participants, it was obvious most of the quizzers were regulars. McIntyre watched from the side-lines as the first round of the quiz commenced – literature! Count me out, he thought to himself as he headed for the exit. This was not a subject he was likely to excel at. He then joined the morning joggers and serious runners for a quick circuit of the track, before heading down to Deck 12.

Most cruise ships dispense with Deck 13 for the simple reason that superstitious passengers may find it makes them feel uncomfortable and also because seafarers generally are more superstitious than most professions.

He did a quick circuit of the buffet restaurant at the rear of the ship. Although it was now past mid-morning, the restaurant was still crowded with passengers having a late breakfast. This was pretty normal on a sea day, when they didn't have to be up and about early to take part in shore excursions. He didn't stay in the restaurant for long, because he tended to find that passengers would look at his uniform and assume that he was one of the officers assigned to the hotel department. This often led to questions or complaints about various aspects of the catering, so unless he was eating there, he kept his visits as short as possible.

After leaving the buffet restaurant, he walked along the open deck towards the bow of the ship where the fitness centre and spa were located. Many of the recliners lining the deck were occupied by passengers wrapped in blankets against the cool sea breeze. Most were reading books, e-readers or playing card games.

As he passed the open-air Neptune Bar, he acknowledged the usual group of regular drinkers who appeared to spend their entire day there. He assumed they had paid for a drinks package, probably premium and were determined to get their money's worth, come what may. The loudest in the group, an overweight male with a cockney accent, shaven-head and sleeve tattoos covering both arms, played to the gallery as he walked past.

'Hey-up, it's the Old Bill,' said Mr Cockney, who obviously had no trouble distinguishing McIntyre's status, unlike the passengers in the buffet restaurant. McIntyre merely smiled and walked on. He made a mental note however to obtain this individual's details, which he could easily do discreetly, by checking his sea pass with the barman. There was something about him which made McIntyre uneasy. Call it policeman's instinct – he wasn't sure what it was.

At the entrance to the spa and fitness centre a couple were seated, having their shoulders massaged by a pair of therapists. He walked past them and stopped by reception, where he chatted briefly with the two beauty consultants behind the desk, one of whom did little to disguise her interest in him. He had seen her before in the crew bar and under normal circumstances, he may have played along with her coy flirtatiousness, but today he was a man on a mission.

He entered the male changing room quietly, peering round the door to see who may be inside, but at that moment it was empty. He used the door marked *crew only* at the rear of the changing room to enter the small office attached to the fitness centre. Almost immediately, he spotted the object of his visit, Craig Leonard. He had his back to McIntyre and was doing bicep curls, with what looked to McIntyre like some seriously heavy weights. He discreetly pointed Leonard out to Scott, the Australian fitness instructor, who was sitting in the office.

'See that guy over there? How long has he been here this morning?'

'Only about ten minutes or so,' Scott replied. 'He's just finished his warm up and if he stays true to form, he'll probably be here for a couple of hours. He's been a regular since day one, but in the last few days he's been like a man possessed. Really going for the burn every time he comes in.'

'Can you do me a favour? When he finishes here, could you let security know?'

Scott nodded. 'He's connected to the missing lady, isn't he? I remember seeing them training together at the beginning of the cruise.'

'Yeah, we just need to tie up a few loose ends with him,' said McIntyre non-committally.

Glancing at his watch, McIntyre continued his tour, calling next on Deck 5, where several of the speciality restaurants were located. In one of the restaurants a sushi demonstration was in progress, but he paid little attention to it, as sushi was a taste he had definitely not acquired.

He then made his way to the casino, which although sporting several gaming tables, manned by bored looking croupiers, was more like an upmarket amusement arcade. Out of the corner of his eye he spotted Dean Ebsworth in his wheelchair, engrossed in one of the many slot machines. He was pleased to see Dean out and about, but right at that moment he didn't really want to speak to him.

Reaching Deck 4, he was surprised by the number of passengers milling around, until he realised that most of the retail outlets were having their end of season sales. Since the ship was repositioning from Europe to the Caribbean, the clothing outlets in particular, were keen to offload any items specific to the ports they had visited over the past seven or eight months. There were also watch and jewellery sales, no doubt targeted at the passengers who would be disembarking in New York.

As he pushed through the crowd, McIntyre stopped dead in his tracks. About twenty metres ahead of him he spotted a woman who bore an uncanny resemblance to Anne Ebsworth, casually dressed in a close-fitting tracksuit. Either it was her, or she had a doppelganger on board. Between himself and the woman, he encountered a particularly dense throng of passengers gathered around one of the clothing displays. By the time he had negotiated this obstacle, the woman had disappeared. Despite spending a few minutes searching, he could find no trace of her.

McIntyre concluded his tour on Deck 3, which housed the base floor of the Grand Atrium, the huge open space midship, where various activities took place. Today it was a salsa class in the main part of the atrium, whilst off to one side, an officers versus guests archery contest was in full swing under the enthusiastic direction of the cruise director. Again, because it was a sea day, a good number of passengers were looking on, not just from the atrium itself but from the various balconies overlooking it. He spent some time scanning the crowd, looking for his recent sighting, but to no avail.

From the Grand Atrium, he was able to move forward into the bottom tier of the ship's theatre where he was just in time to intercept Lewis as he was coming off stage having completed his lecture. He told his colleague he had located Leonard in the fitness centre and was awaiting a call to say when he had finished his workout. He also updated him on his close encounter with the Anne look alike. Whilst Lewis returned to his cabin to change, McIntyre went back to his office, re-energised by his deck round.

20

J ust before midday, McIntyre received a call from Scott in the fitness centre to say Leonard had finished his workout and was in the changing room. He despatched one of his security officers to the location to keep a discreet watch and report on Leonard's movements. About fifteen minutes later, the officer reported he had just followed Leonard back to his stateroom.

By now, McIntyre had been joined by Lewis so they quickly made their way to Room 6201.McIntyre knocked loudly and after a few seconds, Leonard opened the door, dressed in track suit bottoms and a tight tee-shirt. His muscles bulged beneath the short sleeves and he drew himself up to his full height, deliberately emphasising his impressive physique.

'I've been wondering how long it would take for you two to come back,' he muttered, remaining partially behind the door as if he didn't want them to come in.

'There's a couple of things we need to sort out with you Craig, if you don't mind. If it's ok with you, we'll go back down to my office where we were last time?' McIntyre replied.

'I was just going to have some lunch so I hope this won't take too long.'

The trio then made their way to the security complex, before entering the same small interview room they had occupied previously. Once again, Leonard was asked to sit at the far side of the only table in the room, furthest from the door. McIntyre and Lewis had agreed beforehand that Lewis should conduct the interview, since he had established more of a rapport with Leonard on the last occasion they had spoken to him.

'I'm losing track of time here,' Lewis began, deliberately giving the impression of being somewhat disorganised and absent minded.

'I'm trying to remember when we last spoke to you. Can you help me out with that, Craig?'

Andrews spread his arms wide in a negative gesture. His co-operation wasn't going to come easily.

'Calum?' Lewis intoned, as if looking to McIntyre for assistance.

McIntyre went through the charade of looking in his notebook for a few seconds.

'Late Thursday afternoon I believe. Couple of days ago now.'

Andrews relaxed back in his seat and took a sip of water from the bottle he had brought with him. A thin smile played across his lips, as if he couldn't quite believe the two sleuths sitting in front of him couldn't even remember when they last spoke to him.

'Right, it's coming back to me now,' Lewis continued. 'just remind us when you last saw Anne?'

'I told you before,' replied Andrews, becoming slightly irritable. 'if you can't remember, it should be written down in your mate's notebook.'

'It most probably is Craig, but I'd rather hear it from you if you don't mind,' said Lewis, fixing him with a disarming smile.

A slightly confused look spread across Leonard's face. Lewis had obviously unsettled him with his opening gambit. He was beginning to realise that perhaps Lewis wasn't quite so dumb after all.

'It was Tuesday night. I told you all about it last time.'

'Of course, you did. And you definitely haven't seen her, or had any contact since?'

'No, none at all.'

'Have you been trying to contact her?'

'Yeah, I keep texting but I get nothing back.'

Lewis was glad he had said this, because he knew that at some stage it might become necessary to examine Leonard's mobile phone, but for the time being he elected not to allude to it.

'Do you have any theory about what might have happened to her?'

'No idea, mate,' Leonard replied curtly.

'Whilst you were together on Tuesday night, which was the last time you saw her, according to you, did you have any sort of disagreement?'

'No, it was all sweet.'

'During the time you've known her, has she ever told you about any problems she might have, you know, money worries, health, domestic issues, that sort of thing?'

'Well obviously she isn't happy in her marriage, otherwise I wouldn't be here today. As far as I could see, she's pretty well off as she appears to have a fairly good job and money never seems to be a problem.'

'And what about her health?'

'Not sure what you mean. She seems perfectly healthy to

me. In fact, for a woman of her age, I'd say she's in pretty good shape. Should be with a personal trainer like me,' smirked Leonard.

'Have a look at this,' said Lewis abruptly, pushing a copy of the invoice for the Ebsworth party in front of Leonard.

The sudden introduction of the document had a startling effect on Leonard. His feigned indifference to the interview instantly evaporated and the colour drained from his face. He struggled to regain his composure before answering.

'What am I supposed to be looking at?' he said, taking a long swig of water, in an apparent attempt to buy himself some thinking time.

'There's four names on there. Anne, her husband and you and one other, a guy called Lee Andrews.'

Leonard remained silent. Lewis decided to do likewise and a long uneasy silence ensued, before the interrogator finally broke it.

'Tell me what you know about Lee Andrews?' said Lewis, fixing Leonard with an intense stare.

'Look, like I said last time, I'm not sure what grounds you guys have to ask me all these questions. I think you'll find that I don't have to say anymore if I don't want to.'

'That's entirely up to you whether you co-operate with us or not. If you've got nothing to hide, I don't see what the problem is. If you start to go down the no comment route, which I suspect you're thinking about, we might have to seriously consider that you are the prime suspect in Anne's disappearance. After all, you do appear to be the last person seen with her. I'm not sure what the captain will make of that,' Lewis sat back and let his words sink in.

Another lengthy pause ensued; this time broken by Leonard. 'Go on then.'

'Lee Andrews?' said Lewis quizzically.

'First I've heard of him.'

Leonard was now looking distinctly ill at ease. The veins stood out on his neck and he was struggling to control the tremor in his right leg.

'I'll make it easy for you, shall I? We've already spoken to Andrews, several times in fact. His face is in a bit of a mess and according to him, it's all down to you.'

Leonard reached for his water bottle again and took a long swig, draining it completely, before looking up defiantly. He didn't respond. In keeping with his normal tactics, it was obvious he wanted to hear more about what his interrogators knew, before replying.

'Assaulting another passenger on this ship is a serious matter, but I think I know the reason why you did it,' said Lewis, trying to appear sympathetic.' So, when did you find out that Anne had been taking drugs?'

Leonard swallowed hard. 'Tuesday night. I'd noticed she'd been up and down for the past few months. One minute she'd be full of beans, then the next time I'd see her she'd be way down in the dumps. I couldn't figure out what was up and to be honest, it was beginning to piss me off, so on Tuesday night, when I last saw her, I fronted her with it.'

'Carry on.'

'She just came out with it. She told me work was shit, her marriage was shit and life in general was shit. She struggled to tell me at first, but then she just spilled the beans.'

'What exactly did she tell you?'

'That she'd been taking cocaine and some pills on top of that to keep her calm.'

'What was your reaction to that?'

'Totally fucking amazed, to be honest, although looking back now, it all made sense.'

'Did you have a row about it at all?'

'Not right away, but then she tells me that the guy who's been supplying her with drugs is actually on the fucking ship.'

'Who did she say it was?'

'She wouldn't give me a name at first, or tell me anything about who it was, 'cos I think she knew what would happen when I found out. But I managed to get it out of her.'

'How did you manage that?'

'I just kept on about it, until she told me. She'd let the genie out of the bottle, so she knew I wouldn't let it go.'

'Where were you when she told you all this?'

'Down in one of the bars on Deck 5. The Schooner Inn, I think it's called.'

'After you'd had a drink, did you and Anne go back to your stateroom?'

Leonard didn't answer straight away, but instead reached for his water bottle, only to realise it was empty. His crutch had been taken away.

'Only for a few minutes. I didn't get my leg over if that's what you're getting at. By then I wasn't in the mood in any case after what she'd told me. Not about the fact she was taking drugs, although that was bad enough, but the fact that little shit junkie was on the ship.'

'So, would it be right to say that you were pretty pissed off?'

'And some,' Leonard almost spat, clearly reliving the memory.

'So, now you admit that you and Anne did have a bit of a row on Tuesday night?'

'Well, what would you do if your woman had just told you she's been taking drugs and she's brought her supplier along with her?'

'Did it turn violent at all?'

'No. Look, I think I know what you're trying to get at here, but it was just a bit of a shouting match, that's all.'

'What am I trying to get at?'

'That I've done her in or something, lost my rag, whatever.'

'Are you sure that's not what happened? It would be understandable up to a point if you had flipped, after what you'd just been told,' Lewis said calmly, leaving the door open for Leonard to justify his actions if necessary.

'I never laid a hand on her, I swear. We were both pretty upset, but she just left and said she was going back to her cabin.'

'What happened after that?'

'Like I said before, I was more upset with this geezer Andrews than I was with her, so I gave it a few minutes, then went down to his room.'

'What happened then?'

'I banged on the door a few times but I didn't get any answer, which was probably just as well, because it gave me time to calm down a bit.'

'So, you were pretty wound up still?'

'Yeah, you could say that.'

'Can you remember what Anne was wearing when you last saw her?'

'I think I told you last time, it was one of the dress up

nights or whatever they call it, so she was fairly glammed-up. Long blue dress I seem to remember and a silver, sparkly sort of jacket.'

'What about jewellery?'

'She was still wearing her wedding ring and some sort of plain gold bracelet, I think.'

'Was she wearing earrings at all?' Lewis asked, casually.

'She may have been, I can't remember.'

'So, you're absolutely certain you haven't seen or heard from Anne since Tuesday night, after she left your cabin?'

'That's right.'

'After you left Andrews' cabin on the Tuesday night, what did you do next?'

'I went back up to my room and watched a film, then I went to bed about two.'

'Tell me when you eventually caught up with him?'

'The next morning, I went to the gym as usual. On my way back I decided I'd try his room again and this time he answered the door.'

'What happened then?'

'I'm sure he's told you himself.'

'I'd like to hear your version?'

'There wasn't much to it, really. I basically told him his fortune, picked him up and slammed him into the wall. By then, I'd calmed down a lot from the previous night. I'm sure you've noticed, the two of us are built completely differently, so if I'd wanted to, I could have done him a lot of damage.'

'When we spoke to Andrews, he told us you said to him that you knew people on the ship who could make him disappear. What did you mean by that?'

Leonard appeared momentarily startled by the question, but quickly regained his composure.

'I was just trying to put the frighteners on him. I didn't mean anything by it. It was just a throwaway remark.'

'You told us before that you used to be in the Army. Tell us a little bit about that?'

'What exactly do you want to know?' asked Leonard, a little warily.

'Well, what regiment were you in, what rank were you, how long did you serve, did you see much action, that sort of thing? I'm just interested to hear about your army career,' said Lewis, adopting a conversational tone.

'When I first joined, I was in the Royal Green Jackets, but after about five years I applied for a transfer to the Parachute Regiment and I was accepted after passing the selection course.'

'I bet that was a proud moment?' said Lewis, smiling.

'Yeah. Best thing I ever did mate. I was in the Para's for nearly fifteen years and got to the rank of corporal. Did I see any action? You fucking bet I did!'

'Been in a few hot spots, have you?'

'Yeah. In the early days I did a couple of tours of Northern Ireland, which was tough as a Para'. The Paddy's didn't like us at all after the Bloody Sunday thing. Then towards the end of my service I did three tours of Afghanistan.'

'I imagine you saw a fair bit of action out there?' Lewis said, by now genuinely interested to hear of Leonard's exploits. He had a healthy respect for servicemen who had been deployed to combat zones.

'Yeah, I know that's what you join up for really, to see a bit of action, but it done for me in the end,' replied Leonard, a pained expression spreading across his face, as if recalling some unwelcome memories from the past.

'What do you mean?'

'Well, it's a long story, but after I got back home from my third tour of Afghan', I was discharged from the Army.'

'Why was that?'

'Combination of things really. Each time I came back from a tour I found it more difficult to adjust to being back home. By the time I'd got home the last time, I was drinking far too much and getting into fights, that sort of thing. I eventually got nicked for assault in civvie street and went to court. I think the only reason I wasn't locked up for it was because of my army record, but it was enough to get me kicked out of the Regiment.'

'That must have been a real blow after twenty years?'

'Lowest point of my life mate. Anyhow I just drifted for a couple of years, until I was eventually diagnosed with PTSD. Once I knew what was wrong with me had a name, I pulled myself together, got some help and started doing the fitness thing, which is what I'm doing now.'

'So, you've obviously had anger management issues in the past and after what happened with young Andrews, they don't seem to have gone away completely?'

'Look, I know what you're trying to get at,' Leonard replied testily, 'You're trying to make out I lost my temper with Anne and somehow done her in. That's not what happened at all. As for that little junkie piece of trash, I reckon anyone in the same situation would probably have done the same.'

Lewis glanced across the desk at McIntyre, who had elected to remain silent throughout the interview

'Any questions for Craig, before we wrap this up?'

McIntyre shook his head.

'What's going to happen to me now, about the assault thing I mean?' Leonard enquired.

'I'll speak to the captain about that,' McIntyre interjected. 'We've taken steps to ensure it can't happen again. In the meantime, you can carry on as normal for now, but I'd keep a low profile if I was you.'

As McIntyre was escorting Leonard from the security office on the way back up to the passenger decks, he bumped into Kai Rana, the security guard he had previously interrupted arguing with Bahadur Gurung in his office. Rana appeared surprised to see Leonard and stared at him intently. Returning to his office, McIntyre found Rana waiting for him.

'I remember now who that man is, *guruji?*' Rana said.

Guruji was a form of address used by the ex- Gurkhas to denote respect towards someone whom they considered to be in a position of authority. Literally translated it meant *honourable teacher*. When he first joined the ship, the security officers initially addressed McIntyre as *sahib*, but this was something he wasn't comfortable with, as he felt it had colonial overtones. Even when he was a serving police officer, he disliked being addressed as Sir, preferring the more informal Guv.

'Yes, you've seen him on CCTV with the missing lady. Is there a problem with him?'

'A couple of times I've seen him talking to Bahadur. The first time was a couple of days ago, then the last time was yesterday, just outside the fitness centre. They both looked very worried.'

21

McIntyre was still troubled by his earlier experience on Deck 4, where he had spotted the woman he thought bore a striking resemblance to Anne. He spent the next hour or so trawling through CCTV footage of that area in the hope that he could spot her. He was assisted by the fact he knew the exact time and place he had seen her, but the images revealed nothing.

He turned the situation over in his head. Perhaps the intensity of the investigation over the past few days was beginning to play tricks on his mind. But what if it was her? Where had she been for the past few days? Why had she decided to just disappear? Could it be that the train crash that her life had become was too much for her and she was planning a new life elsewhere, a new beginning? It all appeared too illogical, but he still harboured a nagging feeling she may still be alive and on board the ship.

Alone with his thoughts, McIntyre pondered the events of the last few days in his mind. What had initially been a sudden, unexplained disappearance had become something much more complicated, the more he and Lewis had probed the circumstances. If she was dead, had she taken her own life? There were compelling reasons for her to have done so. If not, who else could have been responsible?

The three obvious suspects had been spoken to more than once. Each individual had their own possible motives. Of the three, he felt her husband was the least likely suspect. Of course, Dean now knew that she was cheating on him, taking drugs and probably committing fraud at work, but McIntyre was fairly certain he knew none of those things when he first reported her missing.

They had discovered from her diaries he had been violent towards her in the past however and it was possible that yet another violent episode had taken place, most likely to have been in their stateroom. From the re-enactment he and Lewis had carried out, it was possible, although highly unlikely, he could have disposed of her body over the balcony.

His thoughts turned to Lee Andrews. He was a rather sad and pathetic young man, but at the same time he was street smart and obviously spent a great deal of his miserable life living on his wits. There was no real reason for him to be on board at all. His explanation that Anne didn't want to bring drugs on board herself sounded plausible, but she had been on cruises before and he felt sure she would have been sufficiently aware of the security procedures to know that it wouldn't have been at all difficult for her to have concealed the quantity of drugs needed to last her for two weeks, without them being discovered.

Something at the back of his mind told him there was more to the relationship between Andrews and Anne than they had been able to uncover. Was he perhaps blackmailing her? And if so, why?

Leonard troubled him the most. He was a big, powerfully built man, with a traumatic past and anger management issues.

Was he happy that Anne remained married? How had the sudden revelation she was a drug user affected his state of mind, coupled with the revelation her supplier was on board? He had already shown his violent tendencies with his assault on Andrews.

It was entirely possible he had suffered a similar loss of control when Anne first told him of her habit. Then there were the sightings of him with Bahadur Gurung. More than once, different days. Why were they together? What were they discussing and what was it that appeared to worry them so much?

He had already flagged Gurung up as a source of concern and decided it was now time to speak to him. Although Gurung was on night duty again that evening, he had been in his cabin now for over six hours and it was not unreasonable to wake him. Six hours sleep for a crew member was considered a luxury.

He sent Rana to fetch Gurung and waited for him to arrive. Lewis had returned to the upper decks to enjoy some free time and McIntyre felt his conversation with Gurung should best be conducted alone, since it may involve issues of staff confidentiality. After about ten minutes, Rana returned with his slightly dishevelled compatriot.

'Could you just wait outside for a few minutes, Kai?' McIntyre said. 'I may need to call you back in, so don't go too far.'

He motioned for the nervous looking Gurung to sit down.

Gurung was a short, stockily-built man, about five-foot-five inches tall. He was short by European or American standards but of average height for a Nepalese. Despite his diminutive stature however, he exuded a certain physical presence which was a common feature amongst the majority of the ex-Gurkhas. They were tough, fighting men, hence their long and esteemed history in the British and Indian armies. During his short career as a security officer, McIntyre had worked with a number of different nationalities and found the Nepalese to be the most reliable and hardworking of them all.

'Sorry to drag you out of bed, Bahadur,' McIntyre began, pleasantly. 'There's a couple of things which have been worrying me a bit about you lately and I hope we can clear them up.'

Gurung stared at the floor, averting his gaze.

'Is everything alright with you?'

'Yes *guruji*, no problem,' Gurung mumbled, still staring at the floor.

'Look Bahadur, I hope you know me well enough by now to know you can trust me. I think there's something troubling you. A couple of days ago when I came into the office you were having quite a heated discussion with Kai Rana. Remember that? You left almost as soon as I came in. When I asked Kai what it was all about, he told me he didn't really know, but he said you'd been acting strangely for a couple of days. I've spoken to him since and you still haven't told him what's bothering you. Do you have any problems with your family back home?'

McIntyre knew that to the Nepalis, family was very important and any domestic worries, especially so far from home, could cause considerable distress.

'Everything is good with my family, *guruji*.'

'Last night when you came into the crew bar, you turned around and left as soon as you saw me sitting there with my colleague. At the very least, I would have expected you to have acknowledged the fact I was there.'

Gurung looked uncomfortable and McIntyre felt he knew him well enough to know he would be feeling bad about having been considered disrespectful to his boss.

'I'm sorry, I didn't see you *guruji,*' he muttered unconvincingly.

'Do you know Craig Leonard?' McIntyre asked.

The suddenness of the question, without any lead in, seemed to take Gurung by surprise.

'Who is he?' he replied, lamely.

McIntyre reached into a drawer and slid a still photo of Leonard, taken on embarkation, across the desk.

'That's him there,' he said, tapping the image.

'I don't think so.'

'That's strange, because I've just been told you've been seen speaking to him on at least two separate occasions up on the passenger decks. I've also been told the pair of you looked worried about something. I was hoping you were going to be honest with me Bahadur, but at the moment, it seems as if you are holding something back. You've obviously met this man, so I'll ask you again, what do you know about him?'

Gurung's facial expression suggested an inner turmoil was going on inside his head as to how he should reply. Eventually he broke his silence.

'I'm sorry *guruji,* I do know him. We were both in the Army.'

'Do you mean you served together?'

'No, not in the same regiment.'

'So how did you meet up?'

'It was in Afghanistan. We were both there on Operation Herrick. At the time I was in the second battalion, Royal Gurkha Rifles and he was in the Parachute Regiment. They were part of a battle group operating in Helmand Province and we were there to support them. We were manning a compound in Helmand Province and one day the Para's were sent in to relieve us.

We had to make our way from the compound to the helicopter landing-zone just outside the town. The plan was that as the Para's got off the helicopters, our unit was to get on, to be taken back to Camp Bastion,' Gurung paused, seemingly transported back in his mind to that fateful day.

'Go on,' McIntyre encouraged quietly.

'Leaving the compound was always the most dangerous part of the deployment. Even in the compound itself, we were under fire from the Taliban almost every day. Sometimes we would have to go out on patrol and that was even more dangerous, but that's what we're trained for and Gurkhas are good soldiers. We fear no-one,' he said proudly.

'When we left the compound to go to the landing-zone, I was bringing up the rear of our unit. The Taliban seemed to know in advance we were leaving, because I think some of the Afghan police who shared compound with us must have warned them. We couldn't really trust them.'

Gurung hesitated, as if reluctant to recount the details of what happened next.

'Take your time, Bahadur, I know these were difficult times for you,' McIntyre said quietly.

'We left the compound as fast as we could, as soon as we heard the helicopters were on their final approach. They would only wait on the ground for no longer than a minute, because it was so dangerous. During that one minute the incoming Para's had to disembark with all their kit and we had to get on board. If you weren't on board after a minute, they left without you and you had to remain with the incoming unit.

Almost as soon as we reached the landing-zone, we came under heavy fire from the Taliban, who were obviously expecting us. As the helicopters landed, we gave covering fire whilst the Para's got off. Because I was bringing up the rear of our unit, I was pinned down and unable to reach the last helicopter before it took off.'

'So, they left without you?'

'Yes, they had no option. I was now in a very exposed position and the Taliban seemed to be concentrating a lot of their fire directly on to me. The Para's now had to fight their way back to the compound. They were very professional and very good soldiers, *guruji*. Eventually I was shot in the right leg, although I was able to keep firing.

The Para's could see I'd been hit and shouted at me to run towards them whilst they covered me, but I could hardly move because of my injury. At that point, one of them broke cover and ran about thirty metres over open ground to my position. All the time he was being fired at by the Taliban. As soon as he reached me, he put me over his shoulder and started to run back to his colleagues. We were both hit again, once each, but our body armour saved us from any serious injury. We then fought our way back to the safety of the compound. I owe my life to that soldier, *guruji*. What he did was very brave.'

'Was that soldier Craig Leonard?'

'Yes, *guruji*,' said Gurung quietly.

Even several years after the event, McIntyre could see that recalling it made Bahadur feel emotional.

'I didn't realise that you'd been wounded during your service, Bahadur,' McIntyre continued. 'It seems to me you were pretty brave yourself. How badly injured were you?'

'The bullet passed right through my thigh and I lost quite a lot of blood, but within a day, I'd been medivacked back to Camp Bastion and eventually made a full recovery.'

'When did you find out that it was Craig Leonard who'd saved your life?'

'When we got back to the compound. After the medic had stabilised me and I was waiting to be evacuated, he came to see how I was and introduced himself. I told him I was only alive thanks to him, but he said anyone else would have done the same. That may be so, but he still risked his own life to save me. I can never forget it.'

'Have the two of you kept in touch since then?'

'No. I was taken back to England to recover and by the time I re-joined my regiment, they had returned from Afghanistan. I never saw him again but I was told that he'd been Mentioned in Despatches as a result of his action in saving me, which I was very happy about.'

'So how did you come to meet up here on the ship, if you hadn't seen or been in touch with each other since Afghanistan?'

'I have done a bad thing, *guruji*. I have not followed instructions,' Gurung replied, looking apprehensive.

'Tell me about it. I'm sure we can sort it out.'

'I think it was Wednesday afternoon. I was patrolling on Deck 3, when a passenger told me he'd heard a very loud argument coming from one of the cabins on that deck and it sounded like there was a fight. I can't remember the cabin number, but I made my way there.

As I was walking down the corridor towards the cabin, I saw a man come out and start walking towards me. He seemed in a rush and didn't notice me at first. Almost as soon as he reached me however, I could tell straight away it was Craig. I hadn't seen him for a few years and he had more hair back then but he hasn't really changed that much,' Gurung paused, as if unsure how to continue.

'I'm listening.'

'I looked at him and immediately called out his name. It's a name I'll never forget. He had probably forgotten my name or maybe found it difficult to pronounce, but he just stared back at me and said *Afghanistan,* so I knew he recognised me. We were both very happy to meet again after all this time, but I could tell something was troubling him. He could see I was ship security and I told him I was on my way to investigate a disturbance in the cabin he'd just come out of.'

'Then what happened?'

'He asked if we could go outside, where he would tell me everything. I think we went up to Deck 12 and he told me why he was on the ship in the first place.'

'What did he tell you?'

'He told me it was very complicated, but he'd been invited by his girlfriend who was married and her husband was with her. I asked him how that was possible, but he said the husband was in a wheelchair and didn't get around too well, so they were able to see each other without him knowing.'

'Were you surprised to hear this?'

'Yes and no. I know the sort of lives soldiers lead. Maybe not us Gurkhas, but the British soldiers are different,' Gurung said apologetically, as if afraid of causing offence.

'Carry on.'

'I asked him what had just happened in the cabin back down on Deck 3.'

'What did he say?'

'He said the previous night his girlfriend had told him she was taking drugs and she had also paid for the guy who was supplying them to come on the cruise. He told me he was very angry about this. He found out who this guy was and had gone down to speak to him, to warn him to stay away from his girlfriend.'

'Did you believe that and did he tell you what happened in the cabin?'

'Yes, I believed him, *guruji*. I asked him what had gone on and he just said he'd dealt with it. I asked him exactly what he meant by that and he just smiled at me and said he'd given him the Para's warning.'

'What did you understand that to mean?'

'I thought he'd probably roughed him up a bit and frightened him into staying away from his girlfriend for the rest of the trip. I did ask if he had hurt him, but he said that there was nothing to worry about, the guy was ok.'

'Did you make any attempt to check up on the guy's welfare, or did you just accept Craig's word for it?'

'I didn't check, *guruji*, I'm sorry. I know I should have done, but I trusted Craig to have told me the truth. That's what I meant when I said I hadn't followed instructions.'

McIntyre could see that Gurung appeared deeply troubled by his failure to have reported the incident, particularly since it also involved possible drug offences. However, given the circumstances which had just been outlined to him, he understood why he'd acted like he did, even though he didn't fully agree with it..

'I told you earlier that you'd been seen speaking to him at least twice and that you both looked worried. I presume that was one of the occasions. How many more times have you been in contact with him since then?'

'Only once more, *guruji*. I saw him the following day at the fitness centre, because he told me he worked out there every day.'

'What did you talk about then?'

'We just talked some more about our time in Afghanistan. He also asked me if there had been any problems with the guy from the previous day, but I told him everything was ok.'

'At what point did you become aware his girlfriend was the person who had gone missing?'

'He told me the second time I saw him, at the fitness centre. He said he hadn't seen her for a couple of days, which he thought was strange. I asked what her name was and when he told me, I knew straight away it must be the same person.'

'OK, Bahadur. I'll probably need to speak to you again, but in the meantime, I'm giving you a direct order. I know you probably feel a very special bond with Craig for saving your life, but for the time being I don't want you to have any further contact with him, unless you have my permission. If you happen to accidentally bump into him, anywhere on the ship, just tell him that you've been ordered not to talk to him. If he has a problem with that, he can come and see me. Understood?'

'Yes, *guruji*.'

22

As Gurung left the room, McIntyre sat back to consider what he had just been told. His account of the first meeting with Craig Leonard seemed to tally with Lee Andrews version of events, albeit Andrews had thought the incident took place a day earlier. It seemed likely however that Andrews had got his days mixed up.

He had no reason to doubt Gurung's graphic explanation of how he and Leonard came to know each other. He was dealing with two very brave men, brothers-in- arms, who had been thrown together again in circumstances which neither could have foreseen. At the same time, regardless of the debt which Gurung undoubtedly felt he owed to Leonard, he had a clear duty to deal with the allegation of assault and possible possession of drugs correctly and had failed to do so.

He had only accepted Leonard's word that Andrews hadn't been seriously injured and had made no attempt to check for himself. If Captain Alex was to find out what had happened, there were bound to be serious consequences. Gurung would be disciplined and almost certainly fired for dereliction of duty and McIntyre himself could even face sanction for lack of supervision. For the time being, he decided that the best option was to keep the details of his conversation with Gurung from the captain.

McIntyre then called Kai Rana back into his office and outlined the details of his conversation with Gurung. Although they hadn't served in the same Gurkha battalion together, Rana was aware of the fact Gurung had been seriously wounded in Afghanistan and had almost certainly been saved from death by a British para'.

The fact his saviour was now on board the Enterprise Endeavour however, obviously came as a complete surprise to Rana, as Gurung hadn't mentioned it to him. Rana thought this was extremely odd, as the security staff were a very tight unit and he considered Gurung to be one of his closest friends. His attempts over the past few days to find out what was troubling Gurung had met with no success and he remained concerned about him.

'Do you think it might just be the fact he failed to report the assault involving Leonard that's bothering him?' McIntyre asked.

'He would obviously be really worried about that for sure *guruji*, but I've known him for a long time and I think there's something else, but I just can't get him to tell me,' Rana replied.

'It certainly looked as if something was on his mind, even after he told me about the incident involving Leonard and Andrews. Obviously, I'm really annoyed he's let me down by not reporting the incident, but given the circumstances, I'm willing to cut him a bit of slack. Let's keep it to ourselves for the time being. In the meantime, keep an eye on him.'

After Rana had left, McIntyre was rummaging through his desk drawer, when he came upon a sealed envelope, addressed to him, which he had obviously placed in the drawer some time previously and forgotten about. When he opened it, he saw it was from the purser's office and contained the personal details he had previously requested for the drinker at the Neptune Bar, whom he had dubbed Mr Cockney.

As chief security officer, McIntyre was authorised to access any information regarding a crew member or guest, so long as he provided a legitimate reason for doing so. In this case, McIntyre had intimated he had overheard a conversation between Mr Cockney and some of his fellow drinkers about a robbery.

Of course, no such conversation had taken place, but McIntyre's instincts told him his little white lie may not be a million miles from the truth – sometimes it was necessary to gild the lily somewhat! Looking at the details in front of him, McIntyre could see the passenger went by the name of Terry Little. What really caught his attention however, was Little's address. It was in the same town as the Ebsworth's and Lee Andrews.

Should he read something into this, or was it just coincidence? After all there could be any number of passengers on board from the same town as it wasn't far from Southampton and a large number of the passengers were from the South East corner of England. Nevertheless, it was a snippet of information he would bear in mind and perhaps investigate further if necessary.

It was still early evening, but McIntyre was beginning to feel the strain. As often happened at sea, he was starting to lose track of the days, but he knew that in a little over thirty-six hours, the Enterprise Endeavour would be sailing into New York, the first stop on their way to the sunshine of the Caribbean. He really needed to make sense of Anne's disappearance. From the enquiries he had made so far, had he missed something? Was there anything else that could be done to shed any light on what might have happened?

It was time for an informal de-brief with Mike Lewis. He called him on his stateroom phone and arranged to meet for dinner in La Cantina, a Mexican-themed restaurant, where they served the best steaks on the ship. McIntyre thought it wise to give the crew bar a miss later on, given the captain's cool attitude earlier in the day and besides, he fancied an early night.

As they settled down to their meal, McIntyre reviewed the day's developments with his friend. He was still troubled by the encounter with the Anne look-alike earlier in the day, but Lewis didn't seem to share his belief it could possibly have been her. Lewis almost succeeded in convincing him it would have been nearly impossible for Anne to have remained undetected for several days, with numerous crew members searching for her.

McIntyre then moved on to his conversation with Bahadur Gurung. To Lewis this was an interesting revelation and he was intrigued to hear of the exploits of Gurung and Leonard in Afghanistan. The chances of the two meeting up again on the ship, so long after the event was extremely remote, but against all the odds it had happened.

Of course, Lewis didn't know Gurung and he had no way of gauging whether his strange behaviour was out of character or not. He could see however, it was pre-occupying McIntyre, who also raised the fact that Mr Cockney, or Terry Little as he was now known, lived in the same town as the Ebsworth's and Andrews.

It transpired that Lewis had also noticed Little, as a regular at the Neptune Bar, having spotted him during his daily walks around the jogging track. Like McIntyre, he felt Little may be some sort of underworld figure. He had nothing to substantiate that belief, other than a policeman's instinct. He suggested it would be a good idea to show his embarkation photo to Dean Ebsworth and Lee Andrews to see if either man knew him.

Having finished their meal, both men headed back to the security office to speak to Andrews. He was half asleep on his blue, plastic covered mattress as McIntyre unlocked the door to his spartan cell. McIntyre shook him fully awake and beckoned Andrews to follow him towards the interview room. Andrews looked slightly disorientated but calm as he sat down behind the desk. McIntyre checked the detention log to confirm he was still being prescribed his methadone, which was obviously keeping the worst symptoms of cold turkey at bay.

'How are you feeling now?' McIntyre began.

'Not too bad. Been catching up on a bit of sleep. Not much else to do is there?'

'I just thought we'd let you know that we've spoken to that guy who assaulted you, Craig Leonard and he confirmed everything you said.'

'What's going to happen to him now?'

'We'll leave that to the captain to decide. At the end of the day, a lot may depend on what you want to do about it. I suspect you've got enough on your plate without having to worry about him,' said McIntyre, leaving the door open for Andrews to give his views on what action he wanted taken and would be willing to support.

'As far as I'm concerned, it's done. I suppose all things considered, I probably got what I deserved but he's still a fucking animal. He could have killed me.'

'Yeah well, I think from what you've both told me, he probably stopped pretty far short of that.'

McIntyre was pleased Andrews had more or less intimated that as far as he was concerned, the matter was now closed.

'Do you know this guy?' McIntyre said, changing the subject completely and shoving a copy of Little's photo across the desk.

Andrews studied it closely, but his face betrayed no emotion.

'His face seems a bit familiar, but I can't honestly say I know him. Why, what's he got to do with anything?'

'Just a guy on the ship who comes from the same town as you do. We thought you might know him.'

From Andrews lack of reaction to being shown the photo, McIntyre felt there was little to be gained from pursuing the issue at that particular moment.

'Any news on what's going to happen to me when we get to the States?' Andrews enquired. 'I'm beginning to brick it. I'm not sure if I could handle ten years in one of their nicks.'

The look on his face confirmed that the prospect was seriously troubling him.

'We'll just have to deal with it when we get there. In the meantime, if there's anything else you can tell us which would help find Anne, that would obviously work in your favour.'

'I've already told you everything I know. I really need a leg up right now, so if there was anything else I could help you with, I would.'

A few minutes later they called on Dean Ebsworth in his stateroom and showed him the photo of Little, but, like Andrews, he showed no sign of recognition. By now, Dean seemed resigned to the fact Anne wasn't coming back and it was impossible not to feel sympathy for him. He faced a future beset with ill health, potentially alone. All he wanted now, it seemed, was to find out what had happened, to give himself some closure.

After leaving Dean, they made their way to Deck 14 and stepped out onto the jogging track. As it was now approaching late evening and the usual strong westerly wind was blowing across the open deck, they were the only ones who had ventured outside. On either side, the lights of several ships were clearly visible, further evidence they were nearing the US coast.

'I would suggest a visit to the crew bar, but it's a big day for me tomorrow,' said McIntyre. 'We'll be in New York on Monday morning and there's lots to do to prepare for landing. The Yanks are very hot on immigration procedures so the security department have to be ready for that. I think we've hit a bit of a brick wall with this enquiry unfortunately. I'm not really sure if there's anything else we can do. Any suggestions?'

'I forgot to mention earlier that I've been reading some more of Anne's diary. It appears she's been expecting to get arrested fairly soon, for the fraud at work. The company are due a visit from the auditors shortly after she's due back and she's written in the diary that's when she thinks it'll all come on top. What with that and all her other problems we now know about, I'm really drawn to the conclusion it just got too much for her and she's gone overboard.'

McIntyre listened in silence and shrugged his shoulders as Lewis continued.

'I think the final straw may have come on Tuesday night when she met up with Leonard and told him about her drug taking. We've both seen how he appears to have taken it, which isn't very well, to put it mildly. There's no doubt in my mind they had a pretty heated argument about the issue and when she left his cabin, that's when I think she decided to end it all.'

'That narrows the time scale down pretty much if your theory's correct, but we've gone through as much CCTV footage as we possibly can for that particular period and there's nothing,' McIntyre replied.

'I agree, but CCTV doesn't cover every area of the ship and she could have gone over at a blind spot. If you think back to our position on Tuesday night, it would have been the perfect time to do it. Hundreds of miles from land, pitch dark, fairly rough seas. By now she's probably at the bottom of the ocean and we'll never find out what happened unfortunately.'

McIntyre knew his friend's theory was the most obvious explanation for what had happened and whilst a lingering doubt remained as to the reason for her disappearance, there was no compelling evidence to suggest otherwise.

'I'll speak to Captain Alex tomorrow at morning prayers. I don't think there's anything I can tell him tonight that can't wait. Hopefully he'll come to the same conclusion as you.'

McIntyre wasn't looking forward to the conversation with the captain, since it may call into question the latter's decision not to retrace their route immediately following the report of Anne's disappearance, but that was something he would worry about later. In the meantime, he had much still to do before preparing for the final day of their Atlantic crossing. If he was lucky, he thought to himself, he might be able to fit in a few hours' sleep beforehand.

23

Having slept fitfully for a few hours, McIntyre got up early on Sunday morning. The sea was rougher than it had been for almost the entire crossing and despite his cabin being on one of the lower decks and situated almost midship, he could clearly feel the motion of the massive vessel as it ploughed its way towards landfall.

He switched on the TV and tuned in to the bridge cam. As it was still dark outside there was nothing to see on the screen except the lights at the bow of the ship. Even if it had been daylight however, it was unlikely he would have seen much, as the on-screen data was telling him visibility was poor and they were heading into a Force 7 gale.

After getting showered and dressed, he headed straight for his office and made himself a cup of coffee in the small galley which formed part of the security complex. Apart from himself and the night duty controller, there was no one else about. That would soon change however, as he had called a meeting for all security staff for seven o'clock, in order to prepare for their arrival into New York the following morning.

With a couple of minutes to go to the start of the meeting, everyone was either seated or standing, where space allowed, in the small meeting room. Unusually, the last to arrive was

Bahadur Gurung, who slunk into the back of the room as if hoping not to be noticed. McIntyre could see that he looked dishevelled and unshaven and his eyes were red-rimmed and bloodshot. He looked as though he hadn't slept in days. Whatever was troubling Gurung, McIntyre thought, it was going to have to be resolved one way or another when they got to New York, otherwise he may find himself off the ship.

At the conclusion of the meeting, McIntyre returned to his office to get ready for morning prayers. This was always a nervous time for the participants, particularly on the morning preceding a port call, as Captain Alex liked to be assured everyone was fully prepared. Inefficiency and lack of forward planning were not well received by him.

In addition, of course, McIntyre was going to have to publicly admit defeat in his efforts to trace Anne Ebsworth. He felt he had done everything he possibly could over the course of the last few days, but he was apprehensive about how the captain would perceive his efforts and his professional pride would undoubtedly be wounded.

With a little time to spare, McIntyre set out on his deck round. Having already seen the weather data displayed on the bridge cam in his cabin, he made sure he was wearing his issue anorak and beanie hat, both bearing the Enterprise Endeavour logo. As usual he started at the top and intended to work his way downwards, perhaps snatching a quick breakfast, if time permitted.

As he exited the lift on Deck 15, he found that the automatic doors leading outside were locked and a notice had been placed next to the exit, advising that due to the inclement weather conditions, access to the deck was prohibited. Glancing through the glass doors he could see the deck was deserted and all movable items had been firmly lashed down.

Descending the stairs to Deck 14, he encountered a similar scenario. It wasn't until he got to Deck 12, which was partially enclosed, that he was able to go outside. As soon as he emerged on to the open portion of the deck however, he was almost blown off his feet by the force of the wind. Much to his surprise, he came upon a male passenger in one of the few sheltered spots towards the rear of the deck, wrapped in a couple of plaid blankets, reading a book. The passenger seemed completely oblivious to his presence, so he decided not to disturb him. Whatever he was reading was obviously riveting.

Passing the buffet restaurant on Deck 12, the unmistakeable smell of freshly cooked food assailed his nostrils, making him suddenly feel very hungry. He glanced at his watch and saw that it had only just gone eight, although it felt as though he had already been at work for hours. The restaurant was still surprisingly quiet for a sea day, but he guessed that many of the passengers were taking advantage of a last lie-in before the following morning's early arrival into New York.

Of all the ports he had been to, New York was near the top of the list when it came to passengers wishing to be on deck for the sail-in, eager to see the iconic skyline, so familiar from TV and the movies.

As he made his way to one of the buffet stations, McIntyre was surprised to see Dean Ebsworth in his wheelchair, expertly navigating his way round the various food counters. Dean hadn't noticed him as he was still dressed in his foul weather gear and probably hard to recognise, McIntyre decided to keep a low profile, as he had no news, either good or bad, to impart to Dean.

He was surprised at how well Dean looked compared to the previous encounters he'd had with him. He appeared as though he'd just showered and shaved and was dressed in a crisp white polo shirt bearing the YSL logo, blue tracksuit bottoms and a pair of expensive looking trainers. Judging by the heaped plateful of food on the tray in front of him, there appeared to be little wrong with his appetite. Things appeared to be looking up for Dean.

Having finished his breakfast, McIntyre completed his deck rounds before making his way to the captain's quarters for the final session of morning prayers, before reaching New York. As the participants filed in, McIntyre could feel the added tension in the room as they awaited the arrival of Captain Alex. On the stroke of nine, he strode in purposefully, with a peremptory greeting to the assembled company.

The meeting lasted slightly longer than normal, whilst the captain satisfied himself that preparations for their arrival were fully in hand with each respective department. McIntyre noted with growing unease that Captain Alex did not ask for his report until he had gone round the rest of the room. When his turn came, McIntyre gave his usual update on the readiness of the security department for their first port of call on the cruise.

'I would now like to update you on the search for our missing passenger,' McIntyre continued, glancing quickly at the captain to try to gauge what he may be thinking. The captain's facial expression gave nothing away.

'Unfortunately, despite the best efforts of all of us, we have been unable to trace her. The captain is aware of certain facts which I have been unable to share with you, but the bottom line is that her disappearance remains a mystery. We still have approximately twenty-four hours to go before we reach New York but I don't think the situation is likely to change in that time.'

With that, the captain interjected and thanked the attendees for their input and intimated the meeting was over. He did however motion for McIntyre to stay behind. With just the two of them left in the room, McIntyre tensed himself for what he anticipated would be an uncomfortable exchange.

'I appreciate you and your colleague Mr Lewis have been working very hard on this enquiry,' Captain Alex began, his tone and manner much more conciliatory than McIntyre had been expecting.

'Obviously for me, arriving at our next destination with one less passenger than we left with is a situation that no captain wishes to be placed in. Apart from the human tragedy to all involved, there is the uncertainty of not knowing what may have happened. Could her disappearance have been caused by some fault on board the ship or a by failure of the crew? That's what concerns me. I will obviously have to prepare a full report into the circumstances, so I will need a detailed written account of your investigation by this evening at the latest.'

McIntyre's heart sank at the prospect of the extra work that this request would entail for him, but he had fully expected it.

'When we get to New York,' Captain Alex continued, 'Mr Ebsworth will obviously be leaving the ship I should imagine. Even if he doesn't want to go, which I very much doubt, I think it would be inappropriate for him to remain on board after his wife's disappearance. Are you sure we can definitely rule him out as a suspect?'

'At this stage we have absolutely no evidence to suspect him of anything, but no doubt the US authorities will wish to make their own enquiries, so he would have to be available for them to interview in any case. I'll make the necessary arrangements to have him taken off,' McIntyre replied.

'With regard to the other two men, the one in the brig has committed offences prior to embarkation and whilst on board my ship, so he will definitely have to be handed over to the custody of the appropriate authorities,' Captain Alex continued.

'The other one, the lover, I forget his name. What's the situation with him?'

'Craig Leonard, sir. Again, there is no hard evidence to suggest he has anything to do with Anne's disappearance, although he would be my most likely suspect if she has come to harm, particularly as he still appears to have been the last person seen in her company.'

'Well, in any event I also want him off the ship when we reach New York. If nothing else, he has admitted assaulting another passenger whilst on board, so that gives me ample justification for having him removed. Whilst he's under the control of the US authorities he'll be more readily available for interview into the passenger's disappearance if necessary. In the meantime, I await your full report and we'll speak again before we dock tomorrow morning.'

With that the Captain left the room. McIntyre breathed a huge sigh of relief. He had expected a full-scale interrogation which thankfully hadn't materialised.

24

On his return to the security complex, McIntyre sat down briefly to reflect on the events of the cruise so far. He was overcome by a sense of sadness and acute disappointment that he and his colleagues had been unable to unravel the mystery of Anne's disappearance. Was the answer perhaps hiding in plain sight? Were any of the three possible suspects really involved? If so, what had they overlooked during their investigations?

They had now run out of time however and he conceded it was possible her fate might never be known, which for him, was deeply troubling. In the meantime, he had a comprehensive report to prepare. As he sat as his desk, trying to marshal his thoughts, Lewis contacted him by phone, eager to know how he had fared at morning prayers.

Ten minutes later they were sitting in their favourite coffee bar on Deck 5. Without being asked, Lewis agreed to help him draft the report for the captain as, being a Sunday, he wasn't scheduled to deliver a lecture. McIntyre was immensely relieved at this generous offer, as he knew that Lewis, in his previous role as a Senior Investigating Officer on various murder investigations, was renowned for his concise summation of enquiries far more complex than this.

As they made their way back down to the security complex, McIntyre's pager began to beep incessantly. In certain parts of the ship, mobile phone coverage was patchy, particularly in the lower deck areas, so whoever was trying to contact him needed to do so urgently.

Almost simultaneously, McIntyre felt a jolt of adrenalin as a voice suddenly came over the ship's public address system. Announcements were common place throughout the day on a variety of topics. Most were directed towards the passengers, but occasionally involved crew only. This announcement fell into the latter category.

'Attention all crew, attention all crew. Operation Rising Star. Repeat, Operation Rising Star. Stand by for further instructions.'

Ninety-nine per cent of passengers hearing this apparently random and mundane announcement, delivered in a calm monotone, would have no idea what it meant. Amongst them was Mike Lewis, but McIntyre knew instantly that Operation Rising Star were the code words used to signify that a death on board had occurred.

As McIntyre and Lewis entered the security complex, they were met by Kai Rana, who looked agitated but relieved his boss had finally arrived. More security officers kept arriving from different parts of the ship, anxious to find out what had just happened. A death on board so close to arriving in port needed to be dealt with quickly and with as little disruption to the shipboard routine as possible. Everyone understood that.

'What have we got, Kai? I've just heard the announcement on the PA,' McIntyre asked.

'I think they've found the missing lady, *guruji*. Come.'

With that he led the men into the interview room, where a frightened looking Filipino crewman, in white seaman's overalls, sat with one of the security guards.

'Tell the boss what you have just discovered,' said Rana, motioning to the crewman.

'As you know, we'll be docking in New York tomorrow morning,' began the crewman, who was wearing a name badge on his overalls which read *Jerome Mendoza*. He spoke in heavily accented English, made more difficult to understand because of his obvious state of shock.

'I'm in charge of the team that was sent to check the anchors, to make sure they are ready and in working order.'

He paused and seemed to give an involuntary shudder, as he prepared to recall what he had discovered.

'Go on, Jerome,' said McIntyre quietly, crouching on bended knee next to him, trying to minimise his presence in the company of the much smaller man.

'I went to inspect the chain locker, where I noticed a green tarpaulin which wasn't there last time I looked. I went to fold the tarpaulin away and that's when I saw her lying there. She's dead sir, I know it.'

'Tell me exactly what you saw when you lifted the tarpaulin Jerome?'

'She was a white lady. I'm sure it's the one who's been reported missing. We've all been shown her photograph and asked to look out for her. She had on a long blue dress and a silver jacket. She was lying on her back with her arms folded across her chest. She looked very peaceful, as though she was asleep, but I knew she was dead.'

Jerome's eyes filled with tears and he gulped hard as he tried to control his rising emotions.

'Did you touch her at all, have you moved anything?' McIntyre probed.

'No sir. I immediately got on the radio to the chief engineer who came down straight away. He's still down there now, I think. He told me to report directly to you.'

'OK. I'd like you to take me down there now, Jerome.'

Leaving instructions with Rana to keep all available security staff in readiness in the security complex, McIntyre, accompanied by Lewis and Jerome Mendoza, made their way in the direction of the chain locker.

Although very familiar with all areas of the ship, as his position demanded, McIntyre had only ever been to the chain locker on a couple of occasions. It was located right at the bow of the ship and well below the waterline.

Like most cruise liners of its size, Enterprise Endeavour had two giant sea anchors, one on the port and one on the starboard side of the bow. They were operated from the windlass room. The windlass was a giant winch used to raise and lower the anchors. Each anchor was attached to approximately one thousand feet of steel chain, which was housed in the chain locker directly below the windlass room.

Arriving at the entrance to the chain locker, accessed via a heavy steel watertight door which was open, McIntyre could see a small group of white-overalled seamen, who appeared to be predominantly Filipino. They stood back almost reverentially as he, Lewis and Mendoza stepped across the black-and-yellow chevroned ramp into the confined space.

The chain locker itself was a stark room, dominated by two centrally located spindles which went up through the ceiling towards the windlass room. Coiled around the spindles were the anchor chains, surrounded by a metal barrier. The room itself was dimly lit by a series of bulkhead lights dotted around the grey steel walls.

McIntyre noticed a series of spotlights higher up the walls which he presumed would be illuminated when anchor handling was in operation. He asked for these to be switched on, a request which was swiftly complied with, flooding the room with bright light.

McIntyre was immediately struck by how cold the room was. If it was heated at all, it certainly wasn't at that particular moment and didn't appear to have been for some considerable time.

Entering the chain locker, McIntyre's attention was drawn to his left, where he saw Nikos Dukakis, the Chief Engineer, together with a couple of other officers from the engineering department, whom he vaguely recognised. Almost simultaneously both he and Dukakis proffered a handshake by way of mutual greeting.

McIntyre wasn't exactly sure what compelled him to do so, as it wasn't normal to greet each other in this way, but he guessed it was probably an unconscious gesture of respect for the deceased, who lay on the cold steel floor beneath them.

As Dukakis and the others stepped aside, McIntyre caught his first glimpse of the body. He knew straight away that it was indeed that of Anne Ebsworth. She lay exactly as Mendoza had described, flat on her back, with her arms folded neatly across her chest. Her legs were straight and the long blue dress and sequinned jacket she was dressed in bore no signs to indicate a violent struggle prior to death.

On her left hand which was folded over her right, he could see her wedding ring. A plain, slim yellow metal bracelet hung on her right wrist. To McIntyre, the positioning of the body and the neat arrangement of the clothing in such a strange location was almost ritualistic.

'I take it nothing's been disturbed since you got here, Nikos?' said McIntyre, addressing the sombre looking chief engineer.

'No. I came down as soon as I got the call from Mendoza. I was only a couple of minutes away. We're the only ones who've been in here. Nobody's touched the body as far as I'm aware.'

'Good. My colleague and I will take over from here if that's ok with you, so thank you in the meantime for preserving the scene. I'd be grateful if you could ensure the captain knows I'm here and dealing with the situation.'

A relieved looking Dukakis and his retinue then left the chain locker.

It was now time for McIntyre and Lewis to get to work. Both men knew this was a potential crime scene and they were now in a position they had found themselves in countless times before. With practised efficiency, they got to work.

Firstly, although it was glaringly obvious she was dead, nothing could be done until life had been pronounced extinct. This could only be certified by a qualified medical practitioner. Several minutes later, one of the ship's doctors responded to the urgent call for attendance.

McIntyre was relieved to see Dr Surinder Singh enter the chain locker, carrying a green medical emergency bag. Of the two doctors on board, he had always found her to be the most approachable. In her late thirties, she exuded an air of quiet professionalism.

He was somewhat intrigued by her background, as he detected an unmistakeable, soft Scottish accent. Whilst idly scanning the crew members profiles at the start of the cruise, he had noted her impressive list of qualifications, which made her seem over qualified to be working in her current position. It came as no great surprise to McIntyre however, as he knew that in a crew of this size, there were many enigmas.

Like all other crew members, Dr Singh had been made aware of the missing person several days previously and she seemed to show little surprise at the sight of the body which lay before her.

'What exactly do you need from me? I take it that this is the missing person you've been searching for?' the doctor enquired, walking slowly round the corpse, but not approaching too closely.

'She's only just been found, so no formal identification has yet been made, but yes I'm pretty sure it's her, Anne Ebsworth,' McIntyre replied, helpfully but discreetly reminding the doctor of the deceased's name.

At that moment the ship's photographer arrived, having been summoned by Lewis, who was busy in the background liaising with one of the security officers posted at the door to the chain locker, logging everyone in and out.

'We'll get the photographer to take a few shots of the body in-situ first, so we have a record of exactly the position she was found in, then I need you to formally pronounce life extinct,' McIntyre continued, addressing Dr Singh.

After the photographer had taken various images of the body, including close ups, under McIntyre's direction, the doctor was granted permission to approach the body. McIntyre slipped on a pair of nitrile gloves and prepared to assist her.

Kneeling by the body, she started by feeling for a pulse on the left wrist. She then moved up the same arm to feel for a pulse inside the elbow, before finally feeling for a carotid pulse at the side of the neck.

'I can definitely confirm life extinct; shall we say eleven twenty?' Dr Singh said quietly.

25

Having performed her official duty, Dr Singh took a step back, waiting expectantly for further instructions from McIntyre. Although she knew he was the head of security, she had no idea of his level of experience and competency in dealing with such matters. Even at this early stage, the existence of the body in such a strange location had set alarm bells ringing with her. McIntyre seemed to sense her hesitation as he knelt beside the deceased.

'In a previous existence I was a murder squad detective for many years,' he said, looking up at her by way of reassurance.

'It looks very much to me like she didn't meet her end here. I suspect the body was moved to this location after death, but how and by whom? The only people who could possibly have access to this area would have to be crew members. I'd be grateful if you could examine the body in-situ to see if there is any evidence which could point to the possible cause of death. I'll assist you as much as I can,' McIntyre continued.

As they were about to start their examination, McIntyre glanced up to see Captain Alex standing in the entrance doorway to the chain locker. He briefly left his position by the body to approach the captain.

'First of all, I'm certain it's the missing lady sir,' he began, anticipating the captain's question. 'Dr Singh and I are just going to do a preliminary examination to see if there are any obvious signs which could indicate the cause and possibly the time of death. The situation is all in hand here at the moment. I'll make sure you're kept fully up to date with any developments.'

McIntyre's confident tone and demeanour seemed to reassure the captain, who then quickly left the scene without entering the chain locker.

As he bent back down beside the body which had the head slightly turned to the left, McIntyre looked at the face and head. Her right ear was uncovered but he could see no sign of an earring or stud. He did however notice a small hole in the earlobe, which appeared to be from a piercing,

Gently holding the head on either side of the jaw, he turned it slightly so it was facing directly upwards. As he did so, the long strand of blonde hair which had been covering her left ear fell backwards to reveal a small stud earring. This appeared identical to the one which had been found by the steward in Craig Leonard's stateroom.

'Mike, have a look at this,' McIntyre called out to Lewis who was standing just a few feet away.

'Yes, I think we've got a match,' replied Lewis, who had already spotted McIntyre's discovery and made the link.

Dr Singh looked at both men quizzically, curious as to the object of their interest.

'As you can see, she's missing an earring doc, but we think we know where the other one is. Could be very helpful to us later on,' McIntyre volunteered. He didn't wish to divulge any further information at that stage to avoid clouding her judgment.

'Anything obvious so far from a frontal examination?'

Before answering, the doctor reached into her medical bag and brought out a small hand-held voice recorder.

'I think it's best if I keep a contemporaneous record of my findings, given the circumstances we find ourselves in. I've a feeling it might be needed later on.'

McIntyre nodded his agreement.

Switching on the device, Dr Singh held it up to her mouth and began her summary in measured tones.

'I am looking at the body of a Caucasian female, slim build, aged approximately in her forties. Fully clothed apart from the absence of shoes. Photographs of the body in-situ have been taken in my presence. I note the absence of rigor mortis which would indicate that death may have occurred more than twenty-four hours ago at least. Slim build may also be an inhibiting factor to the presence of rigor. No evidence so far to suggest onset of putrefaction. The temperature at the body site which is currently five degrees centigrade would have a significant effect on the putrefaction process commencing, particularly if that temperature had been maintained over a period of time.'

The doctor paused briefly and switched off the recorder.

'What I'm going to say next may be particularly relevant so you may wish to have your photographer ready.'

She then switched the recorder back on and continued.

'Initial examination of the frontal part of the body reveals evidence of what appears to be faint bruising at the front of the throat, consistent with the application of pressure in that region.'

As the doctor pointed out the bruising, the photographer stepped forward to take his close ups.

Kneeling beside the deceased, Dr Singh then raised both eyelids on the body in turn and switched her recorder back on once more.

'I note the existence of what appears to be petechial haemorrhaging on the inside of both eyelids which is the main indicator of asphyxiation.'

Switching off the recorder once more, the doctor raised both eyelids on the body again, to reveal small pinpricks of blood underneath, which the photographer duly recorded.

'No other injuries appear visible on the front of the body at present,' continued Dr Singh.

'Shall we turn her over, doc?' McIntyre enquired, as Dr Singh straightened up.

Arranging the body in the recovery position, they then turned her on to her front with little difficulty. McIntyre motioned to the photographer- who had previously appeared unflustered, but now looked distinctly squeamish- to photograph the body in its new position.

The cause of his discomfort was now readily apparent. Although the body was still fully clothed, the skin at the back of the neck, the tops of the upper arms and the backs of both legs, where her dress had ridden up with the movement of turning her over, were a livid pink colour with a bluish tinge. To the layman, this looked like evidence of a particularly brutal assault. McIntyre, the watching Lewis and Dr Singh, of course knew differently.

The doctor once more reached for her recorder.

'No obvious signs of injury to the back of the neck, but this could be concealed by evidence of extensive hypostasis on the back of the body, including the neck area. This may be consistent with the body having lain on its back, most probably since the time of death. Colouration of hypostasis and lack of rigor mortis both suggest death occurred at least twenty-four hours ago or more. Other than the bruising to the front of the throat, there appears to be no other visible signs of injury at present.'

Switching off her recorder once more, Dr Singh assisted McIntyre in returning the body to its original position on its back.

'I don't want to put you on the spot doc, but what's your gut feeling about the cause of death, or is it too early for you to give an opinion? You mentioned asphyxiation a moment or so ago.'

'The body would need to be undressed and a full examination carried out before I could even begin to give you a definitive opinion. Given that we're due in New York in a few hours' time it would probably be best just to remove the body to our on-board mortuary in the meantime. Any future examination will have to be conducted by a qualified forensic pathologist in any event.'

McIntyre wasn't in the least surprised by Dr Singh's apparent reluctance to commit herself to the probable cause of death. Long experience had taught him that was what doctors tended to be like in such circumstances. He hadn't even bothered to ask for her opinion on the possible time of death as very few physicians ever committed to such a request. He was therefore surprised at Dr Singh's next utterance.

'I do have considerable experience as an oral-maxillofacial surgeon. As you may or may not know, this branch of surgery specialises in the head and neck area, which I have been able to examine reasonably closely in this case. I've already pointed out the bruising to the throat and the petechial haemorrhages present under the eyelids.

Off the record, I would say that it appears that Anne may have been grabbed tightly by the throat from the front. In some cases, if enough pressure and it doesn't have to be much, is applied to the parasympathetic nervous system via the vagal nerve, it can cause the heart to stop beating and death can be almost instantaneous.'

'The Simpson case,' said McIntyre and Lewis, almost in unison.

'What's that?' queried Dr Singh.

'It was a murder enquiry Mike and I were involved in a few years back, where that was given as the exact cause of death. We only managed to secure a conviction for manslaughter, as the perpetrator's defence was that he hadn't meant to kill.'

Dr Singh's assessment of the possible cause of death, although cautiously given, was more helpful than she could have imagined. McIntyre thanked her for her attendance, before calling for a body bag into which the body would be placed before conveyance to the small mortuary adjacent to the ship's hospital.

He also made a special point of thanking the ship's photographer. More used to taking pictures of happy passengers enjoying their cruise, it was probably the first time he had been asked to photograph a body at a potential murder scene. Despite his obvious discomfort, he had performed well.

In normal circumstances, the entire chain locker area where the body had been discovered would have been preserved as a potential crime scene, pending a police forensic investigation, but McIntyre knew that in a few hours' time the ship's anchors would have to be deployed, making this impossible. Having satisfied themselves they had removed as much evidence from the scene as possible, both he and Lewis returned to the security complex.

26

McIntyre's first task was to update Captain Alex on the outcome of Dr Singh's examination of the body. He made his way to the captain's office. Captain Alex seemed relieved Anne's body had at last been found, but he was obviously saddened at her untimely death and the possibility of foul play. His demeanour brightened however when McIntyre informed him he had a possible suspect, whom he was hoping to speak to very shortly.

Leaving the captain's office, McIntyre called down to the security office for Lewis to re-join him. They had another very important duty to perform.

Several minutes later they were outside the door of Dean Ebsworth's cabin. Delivering what was known in police terminology as a 'death message' was something both men had done many times and in many different circumstances, but it never seemed to get any easier. Receiving no response to loud knocking, McIntyre inserted his security pass into the door receptacle. As they entered, they saw Dean propped up on the bed, several pillows supporting his back, watching a film on the wall-mounted TV.

As the men entered the room, Dean seemed to sense their unease. Perhaps their facial expressions gave it away. McIntyre sat down on the bed beside him, whilst Lewis pulled up a chair.

'There's no easy way to say this Dean, but I'm afraid we've got some bad news for you,' McIntyre said quietly and without any preamble. 'We've found a body which I'm absolutely certain is Anne. There are certain protocols which have to be followed with regards to a positive identification, but unfortunately, it's not good news. I'm very sorry.'

For a brief moment, Dean stared at the two men and said nothing. Then the dam burst. Within seconds his body shook convulsively as the impact of McIntyre's words hit him. At that precise moment there was nothing either McIntyre or Lewis felt able to do. Both fully understood that everyone reacted to grief in their own way. Dean's grief was raw, instant and very visible.

The news he'd just received was probably something he'd been expecting, but seeing it confirmed was painful to watch. After a couple of minutes of uncontrollable sobbing, Dean gradually began to regain some semblance of composure.

'Where did you find her, what happened to her, can I see her?' the words came tumbling out.

'She's only just been found so it's early days yet. We need to piece together exactly what's happened and we're hoping to do that before we get to New York tomorrow. You probably will get to see her eventually, but unfortunately we can't allow that at the moment,' McIntyre replied gently.

'But why? She's my wife, for Christ's sake! Surely I'm entitled to see her?'

Right then, McIntyre didn't have the heart to tell Dean that his wife's body was still technically part of a crime scene and he himself had not been completely ruled out as a suspect.

'Let's just try to get to the bottom of what's happened to her first, then hopefully you can see her as soon as possible.'

'You're not stopping me seeing her because of what she looks like or anything?' Dean continued, seemingly anxious to learn of the condition of his wife's body.

'No, that's not a problem,' replied McIntyre vaguely, careful to give nothing away.

'In the meantime, we have a lot of work to do to piece together exactly what's happened. We'll come back to see you a little later on, when hopefully we can give you a bit more information. If it's ok with you, I'll get the nurse to come up and see you and make sure you're alright. Very sorry again for your loss, Dean.'

With that, both men stood up, shook hands with Dean in a gesture of respect and left the cabin.

Back in the security complex, McIntyre and Lewis sat down to plan their next move. The location in which the body had been found was causing McIntyre some unease, but Dr Singh's cautiously expressed theory as to the cause of death was interesting. This coupled with the earring missing from the body, pointed firmly in one direction – Craig Leonard.

'Leonard has now got to be our number one suspect. I don't know about you Mike, but Dean's reaction back there seemed pretty genuine. If it turns out he had anything to do with his wife's death I would be shocked quite frankly. We need to get hold of Leonard right away.'

Glancing at his watch, McIntyre guessed where the most obvious place would be to find him. Picking up the phone, he called the gym. Fortunately, it was answered by Scott, the Aussie fitness instructor, who already knew of their interest in

Leonard. He confirmed Leonard was in the gym at that very moment.

'I reckon that guy's under one shed load of stress at the moment,' Scott opined. 'He's been doing at least three sessions a day for the last couple of days. Going at it like a maniac.'

Together with Kai Rana and another security guard, they immediately made their way up to the gym, where they quietly entered the instructor's office via the rear door from the men's changing room. Scott pointed to Leonard, who was using a rowing machine in one of the far corners of the gym. He had his back to them, facing the floor -to-ceiling windows, looking out over the grey ocean.

'He's been on that rower for at least forty-five minutes,' Scott continued. 'I had a wander past a few minutes ago and he's got it on full resistance. The man's like a machine.'

Motioning for the others to remain in the office, McIntyre stepped into the gym and strode over towards Leonard. Reaching him, he tapped him lightly on the shoulder. For a few seconds Leonard didn't react but then stopped rowing and straightened up.

'Sorry to interrupt your workout Craig, but I thought you'd like to know we've just found Anne's body. I need you to come with us – now!'

McIntyre's tone suggested refusal was not an option, something which Leonard seemed to quickly acknowledge. As he stood up, McIntyre noticed he appeared bulkier than he had been, even a couple of days previously. A sheen of sweat glistened on his body as he reached for a towel, then took a long swig of water from a small bottle.

'Is it ok if I have a shower first?'

'Yes, but you'll have to make it quick and we're going to be in the changing room with you,' McIntyre replied.

They then led Leonard back into the changing room and stood by whilst he had his shower.

'What was his reaction when you went up to him?' Lewis asked, as they waited for him to get dressed.

'He hasn't said a word about it yet. All he seemed concerned about was having his shower. He didn't seem surprised though when I told him we'd found Anne's body. We'll see how he shapes up when we speak to him.'

A few minutes later they were in the lift on the way back down to the security office. This time, McIntyre made no attempt to hide the fact there were four of them escorting him. The trip down to the office took place in complete silence.

Ensconced once more in the small interview room, McIntyre knew the conversation they were about to have with Leonard was going to be crucial in determining how Anne had met her fate.

27

As McIntyre observed Leonard across the table, he tried to interpret his demeanour, but at that precise moment, Leonard was giving little away. His features were flushed and he was still sweating slightly, but this was more than likely due to the strenuous workout he had just undertaken. McIntyre decided to conduct the interview himself.

With some deliberation, he produced the small plastic evidence bag containing the stud earring, found by the steward in Leonard's cabin and placed it carefully in the middle of the table. He looked intently at Leonard, whose face remained expressionless. After a lengthy pause, McIntyre began.

'A few minutes ago, I told you we'd just found Anne's body. Does that come as a surprise to you?'

'Not really. She's been missing for a few days now, so it's pretty obvious something must have happened to her.'

'Even though I've told you she's dead, you don't seem to be at all curious about what may have happened, where we found her, or anything else. It's almost as if you already knew what happened, as if you've been expecting this. Did you already know she was dead, Craig?'

Leonard gulped and lowered his gaze. His impassive façade was already beginning to crumble.

'How could I?' he croaked; his throat suddenly dry.

'This earring,' said McIntyre, placing his hand on the evidence bag and sliding it across to Leonard. 'Have a good look at it.'

Leonard bent over the table and peered at the object. After examining it briefly, he looked up without comment.

'Have you seen that before?'

Leonard shrugged.

'It was found under the bed in your cabin by your steward, after Anne went missing. It's obviously not yours, is it?'

Leonard shook his head.

'So, whose do you think it is and how do you think it got there?'

'Well, I suppose it must be Anne's. You already know she's been to my cabin quite a few times before she disappeared and, well you know we've been having sex and all that, so it probably came off on one of those occasions.'

'You told us in a previous interview you didn't have sex with her on the last night she was in your cabin, just before she disappeared.'

'That's right, but it could easily have happened on one of the other occasions. She liked me to be a bit rough with her. That was one of her turn-ons.'

'That sounds plausible, except for one thing. When we found her body, she was only wearing one earring. Exactly the same as this one in fact. Women simply don't go out wearing just one earring, especially when they've gone to the trouble of getting dressed up. My guess is, that on the night she died, she was wearing both earrings to begin with.'

Leonard slumped forward and placed his elbows on the table, head in his hands. McIntyre sensed he was ready to crack.

'The bottom line here Craig, is you seem to be the last person to have seen her alive. She's now dead and appears to have met a violent end. Part of her jewellery is found under your bed. You admitted to having had a row about her drug-taking and the fact her dealer was on board. You've also admitted having a short fuse at times, for reasons which may be perfectly understandable.

Now I know at the moment that's all circumstantial, but it's more than enough to place you in the category of the prime suspect for her death. Even if you remain silent now, you'll be handed over to the American police tomorrow morning for further investigation. I think my colleague and I have got to know you a little bit over the last few days and understand your demons, so it might just be better if you unburdened yourself to us first.'

Leonard didn't look up but maintained his position, head down over the desk. Both men noticed his shoulders start to shake slightly.

'I know this is difficult for you Craig, but believe me, you'll feel better if you get it off your chest, especially if you really loved her. I don't think you meant to do it, did you?' interjected Lewis quietly, sensing that a different approach may produce a reaction.

Leonard slowly straightened up and leaned back in his chair, a look of utter dejection etched across his face.

'How can it have come to this?' he murmured quietly.

McIntyre nodded across the table to Lewis, who continued.

'Tell us exactly what happened, Craig?'

'It was more or less what I told you when you spoke to me before. After we went back to my cabin the last time I saw her, she told me about the drugs and the fact her supplier was on the ship.'

'I thought you said that conversation took place in one of the bars?' Lewis intervened.

'That's when she first mentioned it, but she didn't tell me the whole story up to that point. She was pretty reluctant to tell me everything.'

'So, would it be fair to say things got a little heated between you once you got back to your cabin?'

'Yeah, you're right. I was determined to find out a bit more about the dealer, but even at that stage I had no intention of causing her any harm.'

'Go on.'

'At some point I think I grabbed her by the neck and gave her a little shake. The next thing I know, she goes all kind of limp and falls to the floor. At first, I thought she was just kidding, maybe trying to get me off her, because I'm obviously a lot bigger than she is, but then she just remained motionless and I could see she didn't appear to be breathing.'

'Then what happened?'

'Well, at that point I kind of panicked. I'd hardly laid a hand on her but there she was, apparently lifeless. I couldn't believe it. I probably didn't react for a couple of minutes, but then I remembered some of the first aid I'd learned in the army and I started to do some CPR on her, but it was difficult doing the compressions and the breathing on my own. After a few minutes I could see it wasn't working, she just wasn't responding.'

'Why didn't you call the operator on your cabin phone and request assistance?'

'I know now I should have done but as I said, I was just in panic mode.'

'Could it be that you knew you had gone over the top and caused her to stop breathing?'

'To be honest with you, I don't know what I was thinking. I just couldn't process what was happening at all.'

'OK, carry on. What happened then?'

'I just kind of sat there in a daze. After about five or ten minutes, I realised she was dead. I knew I had to do something; I couldn't just leave her lying there.'

'So, what did you do?'

Leonard hesitated, seemingly unwilling to reveal further details.

'Ok, let's take this one step at a time,' Lewis continued. 'Clearly the body was moved from your cabin at some point and taken to the location where it was found. Did you do that by yourself?'

'I don't want to get anyone else into trouble. This is all down to me,' Leonard replied.

'That doesn't really answer the question,' said McIntyre, resuming the role of interviewer. 'Let's cut to the chase. The area where the body was found is out of bounds to passengers and is somewhere not even a lot of crew members would know about. Clearly somebody - and I'm guessing it was a crew member or members - has helped you remove the body to the place where it was found. Is that right?'

Again, Leonard remained silent, his eyes moist with unshed tears.

'We know you have a close connection with at least one member of the crew. In fact, he's one of my staff, a security guard called Bahadur Gurung,' McIntyre continued. 'I know all about it, because I've already spoken to Bahadur about the incident when you went to Andrews' cabin. Did he help you move the body, Craig?'

At that point the tears started to trickle down Leonard's cheeks as he silently nodded his affirmation.

McIntyre felt an overwhelming sense of sadness at this revelation. The suspicion had been formulating in his mind since the start of the interview, but he had desperately hoped it wasn't the case. Suddenly, the reasons for Gurung's strange behaviour over the past few days was becoming ever more apparent.

'Now that we've established that,' McIntyre went on, 'how did you get in touch with him? How exactly did he become involved?'

'Like I've already told you, I was in full on panic mode. I had Bahadur's number in my mobile and I knew he was working nights, so I called him and asked him to come to my cabin.'

'So presumably that's what he did?'

'Yeah, he came down fairly quickly and immediately saw her lying there.'

'Did he ask you what had happened to her?'

'Yeah, he did. I said that we'd had an argument and a bit of a tussle, but I didn't mean to hurt her, but we could both clearly see that she was dead. He told me we had to report it straight away, but I kind of begged him not to. I hate to say this now, but I told him he owed me for saving his life back in Afghanistan, which I don't know if he's told you about.'

McIntyre nodded.

'I know I should have listened to him. It wouldn't have brought her back, but now we're both in deep shit. I shouldn't have dragged Bahadur into this, but I couldn't think of anything else to do at the time.'

'Ok, so what happened next?'

'He kept trying to get me to change my mind, to let him report it, but I guess I kind of emotionally blackmailed him into helping remove her body from my cabin and hiding it.'

'So how did you go about doing that?'

'He went out into the corridor and came back with one of those deep laundry trolleys that the room stewards use. We then...' Leonard's voice faltered as he struggled to maintain his composure. 'We lifted her into the trolley and covered her with some linen which was already there. You know yourself she's not a very big woman, so she was completely hidden. I never saw her again after that,' Leonard finally gave way to his emotions, his honed physique shaking violently as the tears streamed down his drawn features.

'Ok. Just take a minute or two to compose yourself Craig. We're getting there,' McIntyre said quietly, leaning back in his chair, allowing Leonard a little respite. After a couple of minutes complete silence, he continued.

'Where did you take the trolley to when you left your cabin?'

'That I don't know. Bahadur told me to stay in the cabin because it would look suspicious if we were seen together at that time of night. He said he would deal with it and he went off on his own.'

'Do you actually know where the body was found?'

'No, I've got no idea because Bahadur never told me.'

'Have you spoken to him since?'

'I bumped into him by chance, I think it was Friday morning, outside the gym.'

'Did he tell you then what he had done with Anne's body?'

'No, but he was still very worried and said we should report it before we got into even more trouble, but again I persuaded him not to. Apart from helping me move her, he had absolutely nothing to do with this. I've dropped him in it big time.'

'Ok, Craig. From what you've told us, it's obvious you're directly responsible for causing Anne's death, whether you meant to or not. Your situation's not helped by the fact that you failed to obtain medical assistance, then enlisted the help of a third party in order to conceal the body. We've already spoken to you on a number of previous occasions, when you failed to divulge what you've just told us now. For all those reasons, I'm now detaining you on suspicion of unlawfully killing Anne Ebsworth. Do you understand?'

Leonard nodded slowly and stared blankly ahead.

28

A few minutes later, having deposited Leonard in a detention room next to the one occupied by Andrews, McIntyre was preparing to confront Bahadur Gurung, whose world was about to implode. Before he could do so however, Kai Rana burst into his office, an anguished look etched across his weather-beaten features.

'The kukri has gone, *guruji.*'

The urgency in his voice made McIntyre's heart begin to race. He knew only too well what this could mean. The ex-Gurkha security guards had their own unofficial mess, located a couple of doors down from the crew bar.

The centrepiece of this small room was a glass fronted wooden case. Inside the case was a large knife, with a curved blade. The weapon was about eighteen inches in length and was contained within an ornately inscribed metal scabbard. The wooden handle and the blade itself were similarly ornately decorated. This was the *kukri*, the traditional weapon issued to every member of a Gurkha regiment. It held huge significance to the Gurkhas, as both a ceremonial and functional weapon of war.

Knowing the spiritual meaning of the kukri to the Gurkhas, McIntyre turned a blind eye to its presence in the mess, even though the open display of weapons on board ship was strictly forbidden. He fully understood the symbolism that it represented and saw no reason to ban its prominence. Besides, the mess was the exclusive preserve of the ex-Gurkhas and was rarely visited by anyone outside their circle. As far as McIntyre was aware, not even Captain Alex had ever set foot there.

'Come, let me show you,' Rana implored, as if anxious to reinforce the impact of his message.

McIntyre followed Rana to the mess, which was occupied by a handful of worried looking security personnel. The glass door to the display case was half open and he noticed the case was empty except for a small scabbard which appeared to contain two smaller knives. From his knowledge of the kukri, McIntyre knew these were used to sharpen the main blade which was now missing. A small brass plate on top of the cabinet bore the inscription *Kaphar Hunnu Bhanda Marnu Ramro*. This had previously been explained to McIntyre as a Gurkha motto, meaning 'It is better to die than be a coward.'

'When did you last see Bahadur?' McIntyre enquired of the occupants of the room in general.

He was told he had been seen shortly before the coded message to signify the death on board, but no one appeared to have seen him since. Also, he had not been responding to messages on his radio. He also learned that the kukri had been seen in its usual place in the cabinet less than an hour previously.

McIntyre beckoned Rana to follow him as they set off towards Bahadur Gurung's cabin on Deck 3. Arriving at the door, McIntyre knocked loudly but received no response.

Hesitating momentarily, he took a deep breath before

inserting his master pass into the entry system. The door opened about eighteen inches before it appeared to hit an obstruction, preventing it from opening fully. As he peered round the edge of the door, McIntyre's worst fears were realised. A pair of legs protruded from the small bathroom cubicle, located just inside the left-hand side of the door. McIntyre recognised the uniform trousers as identical to those worn by the security guards.

'Stay there for a minute, Kai.'

McIntyre had attended many violent deaths during his long career as a police officer and he was anxious to spare Rana the sight he was sure he was about to witness.

Pushing hard on the door, he managed to squeeze inside the cabin. The door to the bathroom was half open. What appeared to be a male body lay slumped in the shower cubicle, half on its side. The face and chest area were heavily blood-stained and a substantial amount of blood was spattered across the glass of the shower cubicle and in the shower tray itself. Hanging loosely from the right hand of the body, midway down the chest, was a blood-stained knife, which McIntyre instantly recognised from its unique shape as the kukri.

Due to the amount of blood at the scene, he didn't instantly recognise the body, but as he bent down to take a closer look, he could make out the unmistakeable features of Bahadur Gurung, frozen in death.

To the left-hand side of the neck, McIntyre could just make out a couple of shallow cuts, which experience told him were probably what were known as hesitant cuts, common amongst suicide victims. Below these cuts was a much deeper, gaping wound, right across the throat, which had probably proved fatal. From the amount of blood at the scene, McIntyre guessed the fatal cut had severed one or both of the main arteries in the neck.

McIntyre straightened up and addressed the shocked looking Rana, still standing outside in the corridor.

'You don't have to see this Kai, but it's definitely Bahadur I'm afraid. It looks like he's taken his own life and I'm fairly certain I know the reason why. I'll explain later.'

Rana turned away and buried his face in his hands. McIntyre knew he and Bahadur had been close and this, coupled with the fact he still did not understand the reason for his sudden death, was obviously proving hard for him to come to terms with.

McIntyre called for Lewis to join him, as he wanted him to view the body and give his opinion on the probable cause of death. Given the circumstances of the missing kukri and the position of the body within Gurung's own cabin, it seemed fairly obvious his death had occurred by his own hand, but he knew that suicide in this way was unusual amongst people from the Indian sub-continent, to which the Nepalis belonged.

He was unsurprised when Lewis concurred with his belief that there had most probably been no third-party involvement.

A short time later, a visibly shocked looking Dr Singh attended, obviously in a state of disbelief that she had been summoned to the scene of a second violent death in the space of just over an hour. Having checked the body and the surrounding scene and been briefed on the significance of the probable weapon used, her interim conclusion was that death had been caused by self-inflicted wounds, most probably with the use of the kukri.

She also formally pronounced a life extinct for the second

time that day.

Before the body was removed to the mortuary, the unfortunate ship's photographer was called to record the scene. If viewing Anne Ebsworth's corpse had been traumatic for him, this was an ordeal which McIntyre regretted having to put him through. He knew that even a seasoned scenes of crime photographer would probably suffer flashbacks when recalling the bloody scene, particularly the gaping wound to the throat.

The mood was sombre as McIntyre eventually returned to his office with Lewis. He was glad his ex-colleague was with him at that moment, as he knew, without the need for words, Lewis would know just how he felt. He needed a few minutes to compose himself before going to see the captain and of course to confirm to Dean Ebsworth who was responsible for his wife's death.

'I don't know about you, but this feels surreal,' mused McIntyre eventually, half to himself and half to Lewis.

'In the past we'd be celebrating having solved a case like this, but I just feel like there are no winners here. A decent, but troubled woman has had her life cruelly cut short. The guy who did it is probably a bit of a victim too, given what his experience in the army has done to him, but he's going to pay dearly for it. Then we have young Andrews who's going to have to take his chances with the American justice system.

The one who'll probably suffer the most though, is Dean. Life wasn't exactly a bed of roses for him before this happened, but it's certainly not going to get any easier now - and of course there's Bahadur....'

McIntyre's voice trailed off. He had no words to articulate his sorrow at the sudden, tragic end of his colleague, but he knew in his heart that Gurung would have seen no way out of the situation he had reluctantly found himself in. For him, death would have been the only honourable solution.

29

McIntyre found sleep impossible that night. There was simply too much to be done before they docked in New York and his adrenalin was still pumping from the two deaths he had just dealt with, so he remained in the security complex.

Having found out that Leonard was occupying the cell next door to him, Andrews demanded to know why, since he was still fearful of the older man following their previous encounter. McIntyre saw no reason not to tell him, since he knew Andrews would find out soon enough. Andrews didn't take the news well, since he appeared to have genuinely liked Anne, despite having played a prominent part in her demise, knowingly or otherwise.

No doubt emboldened by the fact Leonard could hear but couldn't reach him, Andrews kept up a constant tirade of abuse which went on for hours. It wasn't until he had been given his medication that he finally fell quiet and went to sleep.

Although irritating to McIntyre, Andrews' behaviour seemed to have little effect on Leonard, who remained curled up in a foetal position on his narrow bunk every time McIntyre checked in on him.

Throughout the night, McIntyre dozed fitfully at his desk, when not attending to his duties. Most of the security staff were already at their posts by the early hours of the morning. The mood was sombre and subdued, since they had not only had to deal with the death of a passenger, but also of one of their own colleagues.

McIntyre had addressed them briefly earlier that night but he could see most of his staff were struggling to process what had happened. There was much to be done however prior to docking and activity below decks was gradually being ramped up for the arrival at their first port of call after eight long days at sea.

Meanwhile, up in his cabin, Lewis had set his alarm for five o'clock. In contrast to McIntyre, he had slept well, although not for very long. He knew that unlike in their past relationship, it was his colleague who now bore the burden of events over the past few days and it would fall on McIntyre to deal with the consequences.

Lewis was particularly keen to be up early as he had never sailed into New York before and he didn't want to miss seeing the iconic sights of the great city. In addition, he was leaving the ship at this point to return to England and his luggage was already packed and had been left outside his door overnight.

By around five forty-five, having showered, dressed and made himself a cup of strong black coffee, he left his cabin to make his way upstairs. He noticed his suitcase had already gone and knew it would already be on its way down to the bowels of the ship, as part of the well-orchestrated process of disembarkation.

Lewis decided that Deck 15 would offer the best vantage point to view the sail in to New York and started to make his way upstairs to get there. He was surprised at how busy it already was, but McIntyre had warned him this was one of the most popular destinations in the world to arrive at by ship and most passengers wanted to see it for themselves.

Emerging onto Deck 15, Lewis shivered in the late autumnal chill and was glad he had come dressed for the occasion. He proceeded towards the bow of the ship to the point just in front of the outdoor games court. A throng of passengers was already there and he only just managed to grab himself a place by the rail.

It was still pitch black beyond the lights of the ship and Lewis could just make out the dense Atlantic fog that swirled around them, dancing eerily in and out of the shadows.

Gradually however, a light glow began to appear on the horizon ahead of them as they entered the comparative shelter of New York Bay and this grew brighter with each passing minute. After about thirty minutes the fog began to lift and ahead of them a bright neon glow began to illuminate the morning darkness.

It was then that Lewis saw the first landmark looming ahead of them, a seemingly endless suspension bridge. From his guide book, Lewis knew that this must be the Verrazano-Narrows bridge, linking the New York boroughs of Brooklyn to their right and Staten Island to the left.

As they approached the bridge, excitement mounted amongst the assembled passengers, especially those who had never sailed into New York before, as there seemed no way the giant liner could possibly pass underneath. Lewis found himself virtually holding his breath as the ship slid beneath the centre span of the bridge with what seemed like feet to spare. He could clearly hear the steady hum of the early morning traffic crossing the double deck bridge above them, giving out a sound similar to a swarm of bees.

They were now into the Hudson River and the familiar outline of the New York skyline began to take shape. He had seen it countless times on films and TV, as no doubt had most of the other passengers, but the sense of excitement and wonder all around him was palpable.

Native New Yorkers amongst the passengers were proudly pointing out the well-known landmarks to their fellow cruisers. The excitement seemed to reach a crescendo when the sight that everyone had been straining to see became visible to their left, the unmistakeable, illuminated shape of the Statue of Liberty, standing majestically in the middle of the Hudson on Liberty Island.

He wasn't exactly sure why, but Lewis felt a lump in his throat as he gazed at one of the world's best-known landmarks. Shortly, the familiar skyline of Manhattan seemed to be within touching distance as the Enterprise Endeavour eased gently and expertly into its berth at the Manhattan Cruise Terminal, bringing this part of its journey to an end.

Like Lewis, many of the passengers were disembarking in New York to be replaced by a new group for the Caribbean leg of the cruise. The pier alongside the ship became a hive of feverish activity as baggage was off loaded and new supplies and baggage was brought on board.

Few, if any of the passengers who may have been observing the busy scene would necessarily have noticed the two windowless black vans which reversed up to the cargo bays.

To the crew members working by the loading bays, the sight a few minutes later of a body bag being loaded into one of the vans would have caused only marginally more attention than usual. It was not uncommon for passengers, the elderly in particular, to die on board cruise ships, but word of the circumstances of these two deaths would certainly have been circulating amongst the crew.

This became evident when a second body bag, this time borne by a uniformed security guard at each corner was carried towards the second van. After the body was gently slid into the back of the van, the guards, led by Kai Rana, stepped back smartly to form a perfect line, before saluting, military style, in unison.

Crew members working nearby momentarily stopped what they were doing and bowed their heads in silent respect. They knew.

Of more interest would have been the arrival around the same time of several Port Authority Police Department vehicles, which parked up alongside the ship. About thirty minutes later a couple of police officers emerged from the cargo doors, flanking the slight figure of Andrews, his wrists handcuffed behind his back, before bundling him into the rear of one of the vehicles and driving off.

Several minutes later it was the turn of the manacled figure of Leonard to appear, before being driven off to face his introduction to the American criminal justice system.

Lewis had arranged to meet McIntyre for one last coffee on Deck 5, prior to their parting of the ways. He could see the exhaustion etched on the face of his friend and former colleague. He felt a sense of sadness he was leaving McIntyre behind to pick up the pieces of events over the past few days, but he realised they each had their own lives to lead and both had a choice.

'I'll try to get you a speaking part at any trial if either of them pleads not guilty,' said McIntyre with a smile.

However, he was only half joking as the prospect of them returning to New York for a few days, no doubt being entertained by the NYPD, wasn't to be dismissed lightly.

'In the meantime, here's hoping we meet again. Surely lightning couldn't strike twice, could it?'

ACKNOWLEDGEMENTS

To my wife Netta and our twins Rhianna and Craig for their support and encouragement during the writing process.

To my friends and fellow writers in the International Police Association - Writers Special Interest Group. You set me on the way.

And last but by no means least, to James Essinger, Principal, The Conrad Press, my publisher. Your advice and guidance have been greatly appreciated, as has your firm belief that the most important people in the publication process are the authors.